THE SECRET LIVES OF PEOPLE IN LOVE

THE SECRET LIVES OF PEOPLE IN LOVE

SIMON VAN BOOY

TURTLE POINT PRESS NEW YORK

ISBN-13 978-1-933527-05-5
ISBN-10 1-933527-05-6
LCCN 2006906038

Design and composition by
Wilsted & Taylor Publishing Services

The author and publisher would like
to express their gratitude to Barbara Wersba,
editor of The Bookman Press, who originally
published in 2002 the following four stories in
a collection entitled *Love and the Five Senses*:
"The Reappearance of Strawberries,"
"The World Laughs in Flowers,"
"Snow Falls and Then Disappears,"
and "Everything Is a Beautiful Trick."

"The Reappearance of Strawberries"
first appeared in *The East Hampton Star*.
"Some Bloom in Darkness" first
appeared in *The Gettysburg Review*.
"Where They Hide Is a Mystery"
first appeared in *Connecticut Review*.

To Maddie

Tu m'appelles la Rose
dit la Rose
mais si tu savais
mon vrai nom
je m'effeuillerais
aussitôt

PAUL CLAUDEL
Cent phrases pour éventails

. . . we could all be rejects in a rejected world and never know or dream that simultaneously the chosen flourish elsewhere in a perfect world.

JANET FRAME

The Carpathians

CONTENTS

THE SECRET LIVES OF PEOPLE IN LOVE

LITTLE BIRDS

This morning I woke up and was fifteen years old. Each year is like putting a new coat over all the old ones. Sometimes I reach into the pockets of my childhood and pull things out.

When Michel gets home from his shop he said we are going out to celebrate—maybe to a movie or the McDonald's on boulevard Voltaire. Michel is not my real father. He grew up in Paris and did a spell in prison. I think he was used to being alone, but we've lived together so long now, I'm not sure he could survive without me.

We live in Paris, and I think I was born here, but I may never know for sure. Everyone thinks I'm Chinese, and I look Chinese, but Michel says I'm more French than bread.

It is the afternoon of my birthday, but still the morning of my life. I am walking on the Pont des Arts. It is a small wooden bridge, and Americans sit in colorful knots drinking wine. Even though I'm only fifteen and have not had a girlfriend as such, I can tell who is in love with who when I look at people.

A woman in a wheelchair is being pushed across the bridge by her husband. They are in love. Only the back wheels move across each plank. He tilts the chair toward him as though his body is drinking from hers. I wish he could see her face. She clings to a small cloud of tissue. They look Eastern European. I can tell this because they are well dressed but their clothes are years out of style. I'd like to think this is their first time in Paris. I can imagine him later on, straining to lift her from the chair in their gray hotel room with its withering curtains swollen by wind. I can picture her in his arms. He will set her in the bed as though it were a slow river.

A filthy homeless man is squatting with the American tourists and telling jokes in broken English. He is not looking at the girls' shaved legs but at the unfinished bottle of wine and sullen wedge of cheese. The Americans seem good-natured and pretend to laugh; I suppose the key to a good life is to gently overlook the truth and hope that at any moment we can all be reborn.

The Pont des Arts is wooden, and if you look through the slats, you can see boats passing beneath. Sometimes small bolts of lightning shoot from the boats as tourists take pictures of one another, and sometimes they just aim the cameras at nothing in particular and shoot—I like these kinds of photographs best, not that I have a camera—but if I did, I would randomly take pictures of nothing in particular. How else could you record life as it happens.

Michel works in a shop on the place Pigalle. Outside the shop is a flashing arrow with the word *Sexy* in red neon. Michel has had the shop since I can remember. I am forbidden to visit him there, though some-

2

times I watch him at his desk from the street corner. He likes to read a poet called Giorgio Caproni, who is dead, but Michel says that his words are like little birds that follow him around and sing in his ear.

If you saw Michel, you might cross the street because he has a deep scar that runs from his mouth all the way across his cheek. He told me he got it wrestling crocodiles in Mississippi, but I'm fifteen now and just humor him.

He has a friend called Léon, who sometimes stays the night with us because if he drinks too much, his wife won't let him into the apartment—though he always makes an effort to explain how his wife has beautiful dreams and that he doesn't want to wake her with his clumsiness. One night, while Michel was in the bathroom, Léon told me how Michel's face came to be scarred.

"Before you lived with Michel," he said breathlessly, "there was a terrible fight outside his shop. Naturally Michel rushed outside and tried to break it up." He paused and slid a small bottle of brandy from his shirt pocket. We each took a sip, then he pulled my ear through the brandy fumes to his mouth. "He was trying to save a young prostitute from being beaten, but the police arrived too late and then the idiots arrested Michel—she choked to her death on her own—" But then we heard Michel's footsteps in the hallway and the words disappeared forever, lost in the wilderness of a drunk.

Michel would throttle Léon if he knew that he'd told me this much, because he tries to pretend that I don't know anything and that when I get into the Sorbonne, which is the oldest university in Paris, I'll leave this life behind and visit him only at Christmas with gifts purchased at the finest stores on avenue Montaigne and Champs-Élysées. "You don't even have to wrap them," Michel once marveled. "The girls are happy to do it right there in the shop."

I like to stroll around Notre-Dame, which is on its own private island. I like to see tourists marvel at the curling beauty of the stone frame. It reminds me of a wedding cake that is too beautiful to eat—though perpetually hungry pigeons know the truth, because hundreds of them drip from the dirty white ledges, pecking at the marble with their brittle beaks.

Sometimes tourists go in and pray for things. When I was very young, Michel used to kneel at my bedside when he thought I was asleep. I would hear him praying to God on my behalf. He referred to me as peanut, so I'm not sure if God knew who he was talking about—but if there is a God, then he probably knows everything and that my real name is not peanut.

After smoking on the steps of Notre-Dame and making eyes at an Italian girl posing for her boyfriend, I am now in the Jardin des Plantes. Michel and I have been coming here on Sunday since I can remember. Once I fell asleep on the grass and Michel filled my pockets with flowers. Today I am fifteen and I'm taking stock of my life. Even though I want to go to university and eventually buy Michel a red convertible, when I think of those Sundays in the Jardin des Plantes, I want to do things for people *they* will never forget. Maybe that's the best I can do in life. It is cloudy, but flowers have burst open.

It's amazing how they contain all that color within those thin, withering segments.

* * *

Michel's shop sells videos and now DVDs of mostly naked women having sex with all and sundry. Michel said that sex is sometimes different from love, and he never brings anything home; he said that what happens on the Pigalle, stays on the Pigalle. Sometimes when I watch him from the street, prostitutes walk by and ask me if I'm okay. I tell them I have a friend in the industry, and they laugh and offer me cigarettes. I'm friends with one prostitute in particular, her name is Sandrine and she says she is old enough to be my grandmother. She wears a shiny plastic skirt and very little on top. I can't stand in the doorway with her because it's bad for business. The skin on her legs is like leather, but she is very down-to-earth. She knows Michel and told me that he was once in love with one of the girls, but that nothing ever came of it. I tried to get the name of the girl when I was twelve, hoping that I could bring them together, but Sandrine took my head in her hands and very quietly told me that the girl was dead and that's the end.

I would like to know more about this girl because Michel has never had a girlfriend, so she must have been something special. Sandrine sometimes buys me a book and leaves it with one of the other girls if she's working. The last one she gave me was called *The Man Who Planted Hope and Grew Happiness.*

On this cloudy afternoon of my fifteenth birthday, I can see Michel sitting at the counter reading. If he knew I was here, he would be angry and express it by not talking to me for a day or so. It would put him in no mood to go out tonight, birthday or no birthday. I watch from within a crowd of shadows. Michel is reading. In Michel's books of Caproni's poetry, he has written his own little poems in the margins. Once, in a foolish moment, I opened one of his books and began to read one; he snatched the book from me and it ripped. We were both very upset.

He told me that his poems were not meant for me—that they were little flocks of birds intended to keep the other birds company. When I asked him who the poems were for, his eye pushed out a solitary tear that was rerouted by his scar.

He finishes work in four hours. He'll be expecting to find me at home watching TV ready to go out. He said I can go anywhere I want tonight, but times are hard. I think he has bought me new sneakers because I saw a Nike shoebox under his bed when I was vacuuming. I didn't open it. I like not knowing.

I know he's been saving for this night for the last two months. In the cupboard under the sink is a wine bottle full of money. When neighbors hear glass breaking in Michel's apartment they know someone is having a birthday. The neighbors like him, though it takes everyone a while to get used to his scar and the fact he's been in prison.

We live in the 11th arrondissement. The districts curl around Paris like a snail's shell. Sandrine is not in her doorway yet or perhaps she has already found some business. Michel serves the customers while balancing a cigarette between his lips. He rolls his own and tips back his head to exhale.

Walking home, I always like to pass the Pompidou Centre. If you've never seen it, you may think that it's under construction, but that's the way it was built, and you can see inside through giant glass walls. I like to watch tourists threading their way through its body like ants in a colony. Outside is a gold pot the size of a bread van. No one has ever planted anything in it, so it's probably just for show.

Michel has told me that today's my fifteenth birthday, but he doesn't know for sure. No one does. The story of how we met is an interesting one.

Michel says that before he found me, he was a very bad man, but that I changed all that. On the day he got out of prison, he says he was on the Metro, and I must have been about three—or that's what he says. He says everything happened in a split second. The doors of the train closed, and there I was, looking at him. He says my parents were standing on the platform banging on the glass of the door and screaming. He says I must have stepped onto the train by myself and then the doors closed before they could get to me. I often ask him what my parents look like, and he looks very sad. He says that they were the most elegant people he'd ever seen. He says my mother was an Asian princess and wore the finest furs with lipstick so red her lips seemed to be on fire.

Michel said that her long black hair curled about the edges of her face, as though it were too intimidated by her beauty to go near her features. He says my father was a tall American with one of the most expensive suits that had ever been made. Michel says he looked like a powerful man, but so handsome that his strength played second fiddle. He says they wept and pounded on the glass like children; he says that he had never seen people in so much anguish.

Michel says I began crying as soon as the train started moving and that he remained on the train until the final stop to see what would happen to me. He says he took me home and that I cried for a year about as often as it rained. He says the neighbors came over in one group to find out what was going on. When I was older I became angry with Michel for not finding my parents, and I imagined them living in

7

a palace in New York, which they kept in darkness until they found me, their only child. Michel told me that he searched for them for a week without sleep or food but later discovered they'd been killed in a plane crash outside Buenos Aires. In my wallet I keep a map of Argentina that I ripped out of a library book. Sometimes I trace my finger across the city and wonder where their plane went down.

When I was nine, Michel gave me the option of going into an orphanage but explained how he had grown up in one and they were not pleasant.

I love to ride the Metro, even though gangs of Algerian boys sometimes spit at me. When the train pulls into the station where Michel found me, I often look around frantically. I can't help myself. Michel says they were the finest and gentlest people he had ever seen and that I would grow up to be just like them. One of Sandrine's prostitute friends once said I looked just like Annie Lee, and Sandrine slapped her, which shut her up. Maybe I'll ask Sandrine who Annie Lee was when I'm older.

Our apartment in the 11th is quite basic. All the windows open into a courtyard of other windows. With the lights out, I can see people's lives unfold. A person's life is a slow flash, and I watch my neighbors argue, make up, make love, and fry meat. I can tell that one of my neighbors is unhappy, because he sits by the telephone and sometimes picks it up to make sure he can hear a dial tone, but it never rings when he's at home. Michel says his wife left him, and if there's ever a time I can't think of anyone to pray for, I should pray for him.

I can hear Michel's key churning the lock.

"Happy Birthday, peanut!" are the first words out of his mouth. He kisses me on both cheeks and tells me to get ready. I switch off the television and look for my dirty sneakers behind the door. They're not there. Michel lights a cigarette with a chuckle.

"Go and look under my bed," he says.

I was right, and I shout something from the bedroom so he knows I've found them. He wants to know how they fit. I love the smell of new shoes.

I'm looking forward to having an American hamburger tonight—the same kind my father probably used to relish. Maybe we'll see an American movie. *Men in Black II* is playing all over Paris. As I press Play on my stereo and look at my face in the mirror, I hear a smash from the kitchen and a couple of the neighbors cheer through open windows.

Michel knocks and then pokes his head around the door.

"Prêt?" he says, and I say let's go then.

We walk arm in arm through twilight. Paris never gets too dark, because when natural light dissolves, you're never too far from a streetlamp—and they're often beautiful—set upon tall black stalks, each lamp a glowing pair of white balls in love with its very own length of street. Sometimes, they all flicker to life at the same time, as if together they can hold off darkness.

I can tell that Michel wants to hold my hand, but I'm much too old for that now, and instead he smokes and tells me that no matter where I go in life, I'll be thought highly of.

I wonder if Michel is a famous poet. My teacher at school told me that poets come from all walks of life and that their gift is God-given. I wonder if people will flock to Michel's grave at Père-Lachaise Ceme-

tery a hundred years from now. I wonder if they'll leave their own poems at the foot of his tombstone and then talk to him and maybe thank
him for his little birds, which sing to them in moments of darkness.

Michel pays for the movie tickets with change from the wine bottle.
The girl doesn't seem to mind. Her left eye is off-center. She slides
Michel the tickets without counting the coins. She studies his scar as
we slip past her glass box. Michel hands the tickets to the usher. He
rips them in two. Michel tells me to save the stubs, so I open my wallet and the map of Argentina falls out. Michel quickly picks it up and
looks at it without unfolding it. I snatch it from him and shove it back
into my wallet.

"Peanut's little birds." He laughs.

Then we find our seats in the darkness and disappear into the film.

THE REAPPEARANCE
OF STRAWBERRIES

Eight stories above the infamous rue de Vaugirard, the man in the ninth bed of the Bonnard Hospital ward had requested nothing but strawberries for several days. For most of that Tuesday afternoon all that could be heard were the tiny hands and feet of rain against the window.

While most of the patients disappeared into a medicated sleep, Pierre-Yves lay awake, aware that he was dying. Beside his bed was a bowl of strawberries that he was unable to reach out and touch. Whenever he imagined their sweetness, he remembered her and shuddered. They were piled up in a heavy yellow bowl.

Pierre-Yves breathed deeply in an attempt to bury the scent in his lungs, while outside on the street below he imagined taxis, filled with cigarette smoke, lunging between traffic lights. During his first night in the hospital, after falling over in a square populated by hundreds of pigeons, a memory brushed against him.

As light visits an attic through a crack in the roof, turning the dust to stars, she had appeared, not moments before her death as in dreams, but as he longed to remember her—staring across the river, quiet and charmingly obtuse. He could have taken her to America, he knew that now.

He observed how each raindrop united with its closest other and then, split open by its own weight, ran down the glass in one even corridor. Even after her family was killed, he did nothing—not one thing.

Without memory, he thought, man would be invincible.

As Pierre-Yves lifted himself into the past, he knew that he would not make it back to the present—to the rain and to the ward—but hoped he would make it as far as the garden, which wrapped itself around the cottage and trembled, as summer had trembled and pushed strawberries into the world.

As dusk began to drift through the hospital and unmoor the world with shadows, he remembered when she had told him of her uncle who taught her to ride a bicycle down steps and of the flowers she used to keep in a basket strapped to the handlebars. She had told him this one summer, the hottest either of them had ever known. They had escaped the sultry, slow pulsation of Paris to a small cottage owned by her grandmother. It was the sort of house that appeared to have risen from the earth. Ivy curled across the stone walls in thick vines, and roses sang their way as high as the upstairs window.

The Loire flowed coolly half a kilometer to the west and changed to a tongue of gold when the sun sank beneath randomly dotted haystacks in distant fields.

One afternoon, beside the velvet slowness of the Loire, they had found a meadow and spread a blanket between fists of wildflowers.

Pierre-Yves remembered how she had talked a great deal about when she was a girl. She had explained how when she was very young, she believed that when she stepped in a puddle, a wish was granted. For the slow, lugubrious years after the war, Pierre-Yves never forgot this and would close his umbrella in a rainstorm so he could cry freely as he negotiated a path home.

At that moment, while the hospital ward was dipped in deepest night, he felt a duty to slip away from the meadow and again witness her final moments and the accompanying numbness. Though as the sound of soldiers' boots began to echo, and the smell of burning stung his eyes, he suddenly became aware of a sweet scent, a compelling bouquet hovering around him. The image of the infamous rue de Vaugirard, which was riddled with bullet holes back then, suddenly withdrew, and she was asleep within his sleep, in the garden behind the cottage—a fan of her hair upon his chest.

He watched the rise and fall, seduced by the mystery and delicacy of her weight against him. As the sky swelled and bruises drifted above the garden casting shadows, he picked a strawberry and held it below her nose. She opened her eyes and bit into it. He sensed something lingering and held her tightly.

As the flowers entered the mouth of the storm and began to shrivel, so did Pierre-Yves. And in the early hours of the morning, as he stopped breathing, a recently married nurse who had been watching him since dawn took a strawberry from the heavy yellow bowl and gently slipped it between his lips. In a dull office overlooking the Seine, the nurse's husband was thinking about her elbows, and how they make tiny hollows in the grass as she reads.

AS MUCH BELOW
AS UP ABOVE

I am sitting on a beach, half on my bodyboard and half on the sand. I am surrounded by people who have made little camps with towels and rainbow-colored umbrellas.

It is quite hot, but a cool wind blows from the north. I am in my bathing suit, sitting on a foam bodyboard I bought at the concession stand in the parking lot. My fat hangs down as though it is trying to escape my body. I should exercise, if not to reduce the size of my belly, then for my heart.

The sea looks different in America, but I am still unable to brave the blind laugh of white foam.

All seas are one sea. Every ocean holds hands with another. Although I have a job in Brooklyn, and I even have a girlfriend called Mina, part of my soul is in Russia. If I can brave the sea one last time —just up to my chest—I know that I may be reunited with myself.

I came out to the beach alone today. Mina thinks I am at work. She only knows half the story of what happened so long ago. I suppose I only know half the story, too, as I am alive today and not in that metal case on the seabed. I can honestly tell you that I haven't had a solid night of sleep since the accident. I dream they are all still alive down there, and my brain begins to conjure fantastic ways of rescuing them.

A young couple sit down not far from where I am sitting. The young man is carrying a surfboard. He looks over and nods.

"A little cold with that wind, huh," he says—or asks, because my English is not perfect. I smile broadly and wave as a way of having nothing to say without offending his gesture. You have to do this with Americans because they are friendly, sometimes too much, but this is a noble failing in the culture. I love the summers here and am so white that people must look at me. Mina says I should apply a cream that protects you from the sun, from burning and from the cancer, but I cannot fear something that is not immediately dangerous. Mina calls me a stubborn pig and sometimes she is right, but I am trying to adjust. Sometimes I think my dreams are real memories and my life with Mina must be heaven. Maybe I am in heaven and don't know it.

The young couple next to me have set out some chairs, and some of their friends have arrived. They all look different and are very kind to one another. They seem very happy to be here. A girl with the tattoo of a butterfly on her shoulder has just run down to the sea. She is diving into the waves, which wall up and then crash down upon her submerged body. Some of the young people have smiled at me and I have smiled back. I wonder if they think I am crazy, sitting on a foam bodyboard alone on such a beautiful day. I wonder if they are disgusted by how fat and white I am. I am glad they are close. They distract me from my friends' hands, which poke out from the waves—not calling me back, but waving me off.

If you can imagine bare mountains and a crisp blue sky, then you can see the view from the bedroom I was born in back in Russia. My father worked in a factory that made doors, and our house had the mountains to the back while the front overlooked the leaf-green sea, which was calm and deep. When my father and I used to row out to sea on bright summer mornings, after a mile or so, he would say, "There is as much below as there is above—so don't fall in, my little son."

The farther out we went, the darker the sea became. My father explained how the fish we hauled up from the deep broke the surface like lightning because they had never seen the light. Imagine living in total darkness, until one day you are torn from your world into a beautiful and cold landscape you never imagined existed.

Russia was different when I was a child, and I thought I would work in the same factory as my father. You may not believe me, but to a child, the factory was a beautiful place because there were always thousands of different kinds of doors sitting out in the sun, waiting for the trucks from Moscow.

I used to think when I was very young that each door led to a different village and to a different life. I wondered how many souls would pass through my father's doors in their lifetime, and later, as a teenager, I imagined couples closing the doors and then making love in moonlit rooms.

I was proud of my father's job because it was work for the good of the people. Once I had a dream that I was on an American beach not unlike the one I am on now. In the dream I fell asleep on the hot sand, and when I awoke, the people had all been replaced by my father's doors. Imagine that—a beach with no people, just a thousand doors, all freestanding in their frames.

When the government in Moscow changed, the factory closed, my father died, and I joined the Russian navy.

I think I'm going to ask my girlfriend Mina to marry me. She was born in Florida. She likes to hear the stories about my father, because her own was no good. I think she will say yes, but I shouldn't assume that, because I am gruff with her sometimes, and I find it hard to tell her my true feelings. Out of everyone in the whole world I believe she is the most important person.

The young men next to me are in the water, and the girls are watching. The onshore waves are as big as wardrobes, and I can see that some of the young men are frightened. The girls are frightened, too, but the scene still takes place.

During my first five years in the navy, I was taught how to fire missiles from a submarine. It was exciting because the submarine would shudder with each launch. It was quite an important job because everything had to be perfectly synchronized or the missile would not reach its intended target. On firing days, none of us dared sneak vodka into the launch room.

It wasn't a bad life. I remember having some very nice experiences with my friends in different ports. There were always girls who liked our uniforms more than they liked us. I was so young and nowhere near as fat as I am now. When my submarine was to be decommissioned we

were all quite sad. It was our workplace, after all, and we had grown
quite fond of it.

I met Mina at a Russian restaurant in Queens where I was a bartender. She was there with her friends for a birthday party. They
seemed like very nice American girls, and I enjoyed having their
laughter within earshot. I was fired from my job as a bartender at the
restaurant on the night I met Mina. It was actually because of an incident with Mina's friend, but I didn't mind because Mina had written
her telephone number on a piece of paper and then looked at me with
eyes as big as teacups.

It is strange how some of the Russians I know don't like Americans
but choose to live here. I think that their bitterness has more to do with
themselves and that if they were back in Russia, they would find something there to complain about.

As Mina and her friends drank more and more wine, they became
louder and even knocked a glass off the table. But they were such a
jovial bunch that I didn't mind—it actually reminded me of the long
nights with my comrades, when our K-159 submarine was the pride of
the Russian navy.

When one of the Russian men at the bar began to talk about Mina's
group, I tried not to listen. Mina's friends were not the only people in
the restaurant drinking heavily that night. When the girls ordered coffee and chocolates, one of the drunken men at the bar began saying
sexual things in Russian about Mina and her friends. I went into the
back and washed glasses and tried to forget it because all men become
pigs when they drink.

As the restaurant emptied I went back to my bar and started tidying up for the night. One of Mina's friends wanted one last drink, which I gave to her on the house, because I liked them and hoped they would come back.

As she turned around and started back to the table, the man at the bar who had been saying things took hold of her arm and she spilled the drink. He then began to say terrible sexual things in Russian, but in a smiling way so the woman thought he was being friendly. As she smiled and tolerated his drunkenness, I could not believe what he was saying to her. I poured two drinks and set them down on the bar loudly. I told the man in Russian that he should let her go. He looked at me stupidly, as though he wanted to say something but couldn't remember what.

He knocked back the drink, and then as the woman reached for hers, he grabbed it and tipped its contents down the front of her dress.

He was a grisly man, but remember—I had been in the Russian navy for over ten years, so I picked him up by his throat and dragged him outside. As I was doing it, I remember feeling intense pity for him, but when I went back into the restaurant and saw the woman crying, those feelings went away.

The man shouted things from the street, then went home. He was a friend of the owner, and within ten minutes, the owner himself telephoned and told me to take what I was owed from the till and to never come back. As he shouted through the telephone, about how I was a criminal and a disgrace, I lit a cigarette and watched the prettiest girl of the bunch approach my bar, say thank-you, and begin to write her telephone number on the top of a matchbook. I was reluctant to take it at first, because in the navy I had met many girls who were attracted to violence and they all turned out to be crazy. It was when she looked at me with those teacup eyes that I felt as though she would have given me her number anyway.

Two South American men worked at the restaurant as waiters, and I was friendly with them. They cleaned up the mess, patted me on the back, and said they would have done the same thing. The remaining men at the bar pretended to ignore everything and talked among themselves in hushed voices. They had laughed at the terrible things the man had said and were probably ashamed.

Despite all the fights and heroic acts I performed as a soldier in the Russian navy, I cannot bring myself to take this cheap foam bodyboard and step into the ocean. I am also very thirsty and have a headache. The young men are all back safely from the surf, and because of this I am trying my best not to start weeping—right here on the beach in front of everyone.

All the young men beside me are back safe, and the girls have wrapped them in towels.

A few months after our submarine was decommissioned, we were ordered to tow it out to a given location and then to sink it. By that time we had resigned ourselves to the loss and wanted to get it over with so we could move on to something else. The captain had told us that he was trying his best to keep us together as a unit wherever we were sent. Some of the other units had been sent to fight in the Chechnyan campaign. We had heard rumors of the horrors that were taking place on both sides, but our attitude remained positive: as long as we remained together, we were invincible. There were eight of us in total who drove and fired the submarine. About a hundred other sailors joined us for official cruising, but the eight of us were able to operate it without support. When we had to take the submarine for maintenance, each of us would bring whiskey or vodka down into the metal belly and we would drink a little en route. The captain turned a blind eye. We were one of the only units who could single-handedly operate a sub over short distances. The maintenance men used to call us "a skeleton crew."

I remember the morning of the accident very clearly, so clearly, in fact, it seems strange that I can't intervene and try and stop what happened. The sky was a cold, deep blue, and we could look out to sea for miles. It was freezing cold. We had fish for breakfast. Awaiting orders, we huddled together and smoked.

Dimitri—my best friend—had told us he wanted to get married, and we all thought he was crazy. Several men in yellow overalls waved to us from a tugboat moored a few hundred yards out to sea. They were going to tow us to the given location and, after the sub was sunk, bring us back on their boat. We were supposed to pilot the old sub while it was towed and then climb onto the tug before they detached the line. Even though it was strictly forbidden to drink while on duty, we had several bottles of vodka hidden in our packs so we'd be able to drink a toast to the old boat as it made its way to a watery grave.

As we lined up and were inspected by our superiors, the captain said, "We need a man on the tug to help with the lines." I remember this so clearly.

As I was on the end of the line, he pointed to me and said, "You— go down to the water—there is a boat that will take you to the tug."

I did as I was told, despite my bitter disappointment at being deprived of the last voyage and the farewell drinking.

The men on the tugboat were as tough as any of us. We shook hands and smoked, then watched my friends climb into the sub. It may seem strange, but as the hatch was closed, I felt a tingling at the bottom of my spine, the same feeling I felt as I watched my father—drunk as anything—row out to sea and never come back.

Four hours into our journey, the tugboat bolted ahead violently. I was standing at the front watching the bow cut through the icy black water. When the tug lurched forward, I fell back into some ropes, and although I didn't know it at the time, my arm snapped in two places. When I heard shouting from the stern of the boat, I rushed back, and as I looked out to sea, I saw the towline floating on the surface of the water. After a few minutes of chaos, the captain told us to sit down, that there was nothing we could do, that by now the K-159 was at least a mile deep and still sinking.

I shall never forget the faces of the men on the tug as we all smoked and waited for orders from our superiors. When they looked at me, it was with a softness I had never seen before in men, other than in my father's eyes when I'd wake up in the middle of the night to find him standing over my bed with a candle.

I shall never forget the terrible shame I felt sitting on the tug as my closest friends sank at a terrifying speed.

As if sensing my desire to fall into the sea, two of the tug men came over and placed themselves on either side of me. They gave me vodka and didn't say a word.

As we waited for orders, the captain tried to maintain radio contact, but something must have damaged the equipment, and he only picked up static. Sometimes, when I am driving alone in my car at night, I'll pull off the road into an empty parking lot and tune my car radio to static.

The newspapers claimed the tragedy was simple and nobody was to blame. The line by which the sub was attached had snapped, and the disabled sub had not the power to climb to the surface of the water.

The British sent help almost immediately, but a storm made any rescue attempt impossible. It's hard for anyone to say how long they survived. It would have been pitch-black and freezing cold. The worst thing is that they all would have known that a rescue was impossible.

I wonder what they thought about. I know they mentioned me and were glad I wasn't with them. I wonder if any of them secretly wished that they had been at the end of the line and picked to help on the tug. I bet that Dimitri, my best friend, thanked God for sparing my life. I know he kept a photograph of his girlfriend with him at all times, and I can bet he held it close as he perished.

I've often lain awake while Mina sleeps and prayed for Dimitri to give me a sign that he is okay; perhaps, like the fish my father and I used to yank up from the dark sea, he has found himself reborn in some bright place. I wonder if they drank the vodka— I suppose it would have helped to keep them warm. For Dimitri's funeral, his girlfriend and I, along with his parents, chose some of his personal effects and buried them along with photographs. His mother had watched me throughout the service, which included full naval honors. I know why she looked at me, because I still asked myself the same question.

After the funeral, I told Dimitri's girlfriend what he told us on the morning we set out—that he was going to ask her to marry him. She slapped me and has never spoken to me since. Whatever I did wrong, I hope I can be forgiven.

Mina knows that my best friend was killed back in Russia, but not the whole story. I will tell her one day, and if she holds me tight and thanks God, then I'll know I should definitely marry her and will probably ask her right then and there. I think we can have a nice life together in Queens or on Long Island.

I want to take my bodyboard into the water, not for myself, nor for my comrades, but for Mina. I want to surf along the lip of one of those waves; I want the sea to carry my unceasing love to their still bodies, I want the sea to tell them I've found someone I want to marry and that I have to say good-bye—but that I'll try and keep them going by remembering our good times together—at least for as long as I am alive.

Most of all, I want to believe that being picked to help on the tug was no accident. I want to feel it somehow happened like that because things happen for a reason. I want to believe this more than anything, because if it were just an accident, then God must have died before he could finish the world.

NOT THE SAME SHOES

It was past midnight when he reached the old mine entrance. The rain had stopped. Puddles were silvered by moonlight. Water weighed down clumps of his hair, which sat upon his forehead like small black anchors.

The ground of Edmonson County had not been mined since Kentucky was divided by the Civil War. The structure around the entrance to the mine was a tangle of girders strangled by ivy. There were rotting coal wagons fused by rust to lengths of track.

The air was thick and humid. Plumes of his white breath rose into the darkness. Broken glass, like fallen stars, crunched beneath his shoes. His shoes—full of holes—were the shoes she had plucked from the shop shelf years ago.

"How handsome," she had said all those years ago at the store. He had stood at the mirror slightly bowlegged, his eyes askew as they both peered at the crooked body to which the shoes were attached.

"How handsome in those shoes," she had said as they bounced their way home in the truck, such a long time ago.

He bent his way past the old bunkers, farther into the night, past ghost miners gossiping over tin cups. He remembered the photographs she kept under her bed, the honey-colored portraits of ancestors. Welsh choirs, bearded men in tunics, and women's heads poking out from rings of white linen, coal-dusted cheeks against leaden skies, the first car in town, gas lamps in doorways.

He stepped over a collapsed wall. He continued walking until the rocks and broken glass beneath became a carpet of grass and then a meadow. The meadow sloped unevenly toward a river, as though slowly tipping its contents into the gushing tongue of water.

He stopped here and listened.

The low hissing of the river. His own breathing. Wind rushing between stems of wet grass.

They had just spent that afternoon together, soaking each other up after six years of not one word. No matter where he went, he had been unable to escape Edmonson County because it was her home and it haunted him; the fiddling of crickets; the smell of a hot night; a clear, cool pond—his senses had conspired to bring him back.

Now, on a sloping meadow hours into a fresh day, he found himself a desperate man, struggling to free himself from the shackles of a life he had not pursued. And her voice trickled through him, an icicle perpetually melting.

She was curiously delighted to see him that day when he showed up after six years. She was working at the same place. She did not act surprised, as if for all that time he had been hiding somewhere close by. They drove through town in her small truck. Roofs were being hammered, children kicked stones, she slipped off her shoes to drive.

In the country not far from her house, a heavy pink mist swallowed up the legs of cows and the trunks of trees. After miles along dusty narrow roads, they pulled into her driveway and parked next to a claw-foot bathtub filled with dry leaves. Several dogs scrambled off the porch tossing their limbs and barking. They ran in circles around the truck.

He watched her walk barefoot across the driveway and then followed her into the house. As he stepped onto the porch, a line of cats' heads appeared at the screen door and then disappeared when the thunder of dogs approached.

As he peeled open the screen door, he noticed small cats poised before him, watching his movements intently, as if he had inadvertently set foot upon the stage of a feline theater. The cats lounged on shelves, atop the refrigerator, and on stairs. Like strange mechanical toys, they raised their paws and swiveled their heads. The ones adrift on the floor were curled up and listened to their mistress in the kitchen as she skated a tall spoon around a glass of iced tea. The dogs bounded toward him again, salivating. Several of the cats were trodden on and hissed.

She stirred the iced tea and sang. Then he stirred it as she sat down and asked questions about his life. He stirred the tea until they were both silent—as though from its sugary bottom, something delicate had risen and usurped language.

Neither of them was married, and this gave the illusion that little had changed. With the glass of iced tea in his hand, he almost confessed everything.

Years ago, they were engaged to be married, but one day he left.

He forgot why he had left long before he realized that she could not be forgotten, that the boundary of their intimacy was impossible to cross.

Displayed on a lone shelf with English paperback novels was an old pickax with her granddaddy's initials, M.L. He contemplated that he was sitting on top of the him that had never left—a him that had not been away for six years, a him that was running over in his head how much money the tobacco crop might yield and how much help he would need hanging it.

In between talk were pockets of silence, in which he mused upon the confusing dichotomy before him. How easy, he thought, it would be to stay, to make this my chair. How accustomed I could become to the animals, why, after a day or so I would know their names and could call them for supper. He peered out to the porch and saw how it could be improved—making a mental note of tools for the job.

It was soon time to feed the dogs, and he offered to help—a way to continue the illusion of an everyday life. When the biggest dog rose from crusty folds of blankets, there lay a pair of shoes, a little chewed but intact. As he pulled them out, he remembered how she had chosen them in the shop.

She saw him holding them and turned away.

"They're not the same shoes," she said.

"They sure look the same—the ones you picked out."

"Not those, honey." The words shivered as they fell from her mouth. "They're not yours anymore."

After slipping the shoes onto his feet, replacing them with the ones he'd arrived in as a gesture of fairness, the light in the house dimmed and he followed her singing to the backyard. She was standing beside a tree from which two swings hung off the same branch.

"Swing," she said sadly, the hard blue of her eyes glistening. And so they swung for their lives, the end of the branch above like an old finger, cutting out a circle of dusk.

As morning flooded the meadow below with light and then shape, he pictured her back at the house asleep on the porch in a rocker, golden cords of her hair adrift on bare shoulders.

They are the same shoes, he thought, the ones she picked.

And he listened because wind was filling the old mine as though deep underground in silence and in darkness, the earth once more had grown rich and waited for the clumsy but devoted hands of men.

WHERE THEY HIDE
IS A MYSTERY

Since his mother's funeral, Edgar had begun to walk alone through the park. When he was a baby, she pushed him along its many paths. In the afternoons she read books to him, and though he couldn't talk then, she knew he was listening, and he remembered her voice. When she died, his childhood split open beneath his feet.

His father, a handsome, stern man who smelled of smoke and cologne, had forbidden Edgar to leave the apartment without a grown-up, but his father generally stayed at the office until late into the night. Edgar knew he would not be missed.

Slipping out past Stan the doorman was not difficult. Stan liked a drink and would disappear every couple of hours for fifteen minutes, after which he'd sit in his room and try to appear as sober as possible, which made him look even more drunk.

Once Edgar crossed Fifth Avenue, he followed a path far into the woods. On entering the park, he often saw tourists having their portraits made, fire jugglers, slow games of chess, forlorn secretaries, and the homeless who gathered in groups to debate the weather in loud voices.

Nestled between a sycamore tree and a cluster of lilac bushes, there was a bench where his mother had told him secrets.

"Without you," she had once said, "the world would be incomplete."

The bench was not particularly ornate. It was small and wooden and in the rain would soften and grow dark.

Edgar had overheard his father say on the telephone that he would never get over his wife's death but that he would just learn to live with it. Stan the doorman had told Edgar that she was in a better place, but Edgar could not imagine anywhere better than the park, especially in spring when the lilacs—like tiny bombs—burst open and spill their fragrance upon a carpet of crabgrass.

Around the legs of the bench were clusters of tea-rose bushes, which his mother called Peter Pan roses, on account of their refusal to grow into the soft, many-layered cups of their cousins.

Not long after she was diagnosed, she would—despite the doctors' instructions—sneak out with Edgar, and they would stroll very slowly through the park. After three months, she could only walk with the help of a cane, and as she walked, she balanced upon it like a tired acrobat. When her wrists and ankles grew tiny and she could no longer leave the apartment, Edgar wrapped the cane in Christmas paper and put it under his bed. It had bent slightly by supporting her. It was crooked with the weight of her love.

A week after she died, Edgar was awakened by the sound of his father cleaning out her closet. Through a cracked bedroom door, he watched his father angrily scoop out her sweaters, skirts, underwear, and socks, and then put them into trash bags. On his walks through the park after school, Edgar would remember the sound clothes hangers had made sliding across the pole of her closet, and the breathlessness of his father—the agony of being left behind.

Edgar was angry with his father for disposing of his mother's clothes as if they were copies of old Sunday papers, but they never exchanged any words about it; in fact, they never spoke to one another except about school or work.

The morning after his father cleared everything out, Edgar had untied the string on one of the bags and rescued a sweater. It was under his bed with the cane and a birthday present he had been unable to open. A small card attached to the gift read: "I know you won't forget me."

On the wrapping paper were drawings of Peter Pan roses.

Edgar drifted farther away from his father. They communicated through silence that flowed between them like a river. In the months that followed her death, the river widened, until Edgar's father was a motionless speck in a wrinkled suit watching him, arms akimbo, from the opposite bank.

Sneaking out past Stan the doorman, and then sinking into the lush green of the park was the only activity that bore any significance for Edgar. He ate to keep himself from feeling dizzy, and he slept so that he would not fall asleep during the lugubrious activities of daily life.

School was an ordered dream. He paid attention in class and he ate lunch with the other children, but their laughter only reminded him of how unlucky his mother had been. When invited over to play at other boys' houses, he quietly declined.

Edgar had taken on the life of a shadow, while his true self—like a stone figure of Narnia—remained at the bedside of his shrinking mother.

Christmas came and went. Stan the doorman brought in a tree and helped Edgar's father string lights through its branches. Presents arrived and were opened. A turkey was carved, but joy had regressed into the trunks of the trees, and into the sleeping bombs of the lilacs.

Edgar's father acquired a dog, which Stan offered to walk but seldom did. Like a piano bought for the purpose of decoration, the dog somehow knew that no true pleasure was taken from its presence and it spent most of the day and night in its bed, and then one day it disappeared and nobody noticed.

Edgar's father began to work every other Saturday, and then every Saturday. The apartment fell asleep under dust. Life became quiet and drawn out like a wet Sunday afternoon. By the time winter passed and the earth began to soften, the river of silence between Edgar and his father had become a sea—but it was not rough, nor did the tides bring news of change. Beneath the surface swam unsaid things.

On the one-year anniversary of her death, Edgar's father left the apartment before Edgar woke up. One hour before the car arrived to take Edgar to school, he made himself some cereal and then pulled her sweater from under the bed. He folded it, and by removing his homework and a history book, he found a space for it in his backpack. The scent of her sweater almost drove him mad, and during recess, he found an empty cubicle in the bathroom, opened his bag, and inhaled what little of her life it had absorbed.

After school as usual, he crossed Fifth Avenue and headed for the bench. Along the main path, a tourist laughed uncontrollably as he posed for a portrait. His girlfriend laughed, too; they kissed. At first, Edgar had thought tourists were foolish to want pictures for themselves and their loved ones, but after his mother died, he realized that memory needs all the help it can get, and things are sometimes like keys.

When Edgar arrived at the end of the grove that hid the bench, the scent of lilacs picked him up and carried him forward, but then he stopped because there was a man on the bench with his eyes closed.

The man was Indian and had a turban tied around his head. He wore a brown suit and a stiff raincoat stained with water marks.

The turban was almost the same color as his suit, and bits of thread dangled from it like the beads that sometimes hang from lampshades.

As Edgar approached, the man opened his eyes and peered up at him.

"I'm sorry," Edgar commanded, "but you can't sit here."

The man adjusted the turban slightly. One of his eyes began to wander to the side of its socket, as though it yearned for a life of its own.

"I can't sit here?" he said.

"I didn't know anyone knew about this place," Edgar said, looking back upon the path.

"Oh, I think it would be very popular," said the man. "It's lovely."

Edgar sensed that the man had no intention of leaving and so climbed up onto the bench beside him.

"How do you know about this place then, if it is such a very big secret?" The man leaned into a purple nose of lilacs and sniffed.

"My mother used to bring me here," Edgar said.

"Oh?" he said, though this time, he seemed surprised. "She's not here today?"

"She's dead," Edgar said.

The man began to laugh and then jumped off the bench.

"You must be crazy!" he said, adjusting the turban on his head. "People don't die!" He laughed again, though not mockingly, but with utter incredulity.

The man's loose eye drifted in its socket, while the obedient one remained fixed on Edgar.

"You must be crazy," the man said again, sitting back down on the bench. Edgar shrank back and looked up at a small opening in the trees. It had clouded over, but the vegetation around him swelled.

"You're not scared of me, are you?" the man asked.

"No," Edgar replied. He was not scared because he felt that life had already done its worst.

"Well, don't worry about my terrible eye." The man pointed. "It sees everything quite clearly when it wants to."

"But I was with her when she died," Edgar said.

"Stop talking crazy," the man insisted, which made Edgar cry.

The sky darkened suddenly, and a soft wind shook the bloated ends of the lilac trees.

"Could it be that your mother is actually here? With us now?" the man asked softly. "Your tears are falling upon her small hands," he said, kneeling down at Edgar's feet. He cradled a wet tea-rose leaf in his hand. "See?"

Edgar looked down and imagined the fragrant cups of roses, which in summer would pop open around the bench. He remembered his mother's fascination for small things.

"It's just a Peter Pan rose," Edgar said.

The man laughed, and his eye slipped from its moorings. "And I suppose that the wind is just air? And not laughter's laughter?"

"I wish I could believe you," Edgar said.

"Terrible." The Indian man shook his head.

"I don't understand how she could leave us," Edgar said.

"I know, it's awful."

"Why did it have to happen?" Edgar asked.

"She's just changed clothes."

Edgar imagined repeating all this to his father—the ensuing sigh, and then the click of the door as his body made a quiet exit.

"If you think she has gone for good, then you're cutting yourself short, my friend," the man said. He pulled an orange from his pocket and began to peel away its skin with his nail.

"My own wife," the man said with a mouthful of orange, "is the blend of light in late summer that pushes through the smoky trees to the soft fists of windfallen apples. Would you like some orange?"

"No thanks."

"Oh, you really should, it's rare you find such a sweet one," the man said. "And I can tell that you haven't been eating."

Edgar shuffled in his seat.

"What would your mother say?" He held out a segment of orange. Clouds above them broke apart and trees echoed with birdsong.

Edgar and the man chewed silently.

"I'm very sorry," the man said when they had finished the orange.

"My father threw away all her clothes."

"That's not uncommon."

"Why?" Edgar asked.

The man turned to Edgar. "He probably hasn't said much to you either, has he?"

"No, he just works, and then when he does come home before I go to bed we have dinner, and then I go to my room while he reads the newspaper."

"And I suppose you think that he doesn't love you?"

Edgar nodded.

"Big problem," the man said to himself.

"What is?" Edgar asked.

"Well, he loves you both so much that it consumes him." The man's loose eye began to revolve. "When somebody leaves this plane—or, if you like, goes into another room—those left behind sometimes try and stop loving—but this is a mistake, because even if you have loved only once in your life, you're ruined."

Edgar imagined the sad, bent figure of his father.

"Before I met with my wife, I loved her very much. I didn't know who she was, but I had this fire inside me for someone I knew existed. Now that she hangs out stars, I still love her, though we speak another language altogether."

"Is she dead, too?" Edgar asked.

"Are you listening to a word I'm saying?"

"Sorry."

"Okay, you're forgiven, but no more of this silliness."

A bird dipped between the trees and came to rest on a branch.

"You have to help your father."

Edgar imagined his father at the office, the dark rings beneath his eyes. The beauty of his slowness.

In the early stages of his mother's illness, Edgar had secretly watched his father get down on his knees and gather up the clumps of her hair from the shower drain. Before anyone truly believed what would happen, Edgar's father had tried to save everything, and he kept the hair in a pillowcase.

"Come," the man said. "This is a very pleasant seat, but let's go for a walk."

Edgar didn't move.

"Show me all the places she took you. Let's ride on the subway and sing her favorite song."

Edgar couldn't think of anything to say. His mother had told him never to talk to strangers.

"I know that you might be afraid—what I'm saying is hard to believe, but it's possible to continue loving, if you know how."

Edgar felt for the sweater in his bag.

"You are hungry and so am I," the man said, rubbing his chin, as though it had suddenly appeared on his face. Adjusting his turban, he said, "Okay, I have a very nice suggestion. You are going to tell me the favorite eating place of your mother, and then I am going to go to the favorite eating place of your mother, and if you like, you can join me there."

Edgar told him about a Chinese restaurant on the Lower East Side, and then the man walked to the end of the grove and was gone.

One whole year—365 days ago, her eyes had closed and her hand (which had shrunk until it was almost the same size as Edgar's) released her son's hand. Her soul, like a spring coiled between two doors, was vaulted into the unknowable as one door opened.

A boy at school had told him there was no such thing as a soul, that people were just machines. And even though the boy had meant no harm and everything he said made sense, Edgar felt as though there was some information that had been withheld, not only from the boy, but from everyone.

Moments before his mother died, Edgar remembered a sudden energy had filled her. For several minutes, her eyes opened very wide. She even tried to sit up. She looked around the room and then at Edgar's father, who sat—frozen with disbelief—at the end of her bed.

Anniversaries are sad and beautiful. Snow momentarily turns to rain.

Edgar pushed open the door of the Chinese restaurant—advertisements flapped upon its door like wings.

He slid into the booth opposite the man, whose loose eye was following the waiter back to the kitchen.

When Edgar sat down, a Chinese woman appeared through a bead curtain.

"Long time since you come, Edgar."

"Yes," Edgar said, and felt his mother warm his insides.

The Indian man cupped his hand on Edgar's shoulder.

Edgar ordered all the dishes his mother had loved. Moo shu pork, pork-fried rice, hot and sour soup, won ton crispy duck, and General Tso's chicken.

There was a fish tank opposite their booth, and Edgar wondered if the fish remembered them.

It was a strange thing to taste all her favorite foods. The smell of the duck and the thick smoothness of the soup all conjured her.

He could see her long fingers on the table, occasionally scooping steaming food onto his plate. She pushed her strawberry blonde hair behind her ears, and her eyes widened with each mouthful. They discussed school, the importance of nutrition, and where they would go for a vacation in August when New York was unbearably sticky.

The strange man opposite Edgar ate in silence.

After the meal, the Indian man scooped out handfuls of quarters from his pocket. The Chinese woman counted them on the bar loudly.

Edgar opened his fortune cookie. He broke the stale biscuit and read it to himself. It said:

"Long Roots Moor Love to Our Side"

Next, they went to a Laundromat in Chelsea and sat in orange, molded chairs beside churning washers. It was late, but Edgar knew that his father would not be home yet.

"Even though we always had a laundry service," Edgar said, "Mommy used to bring me here for fun."

The Indian man nodded. Several Polish women folded towels next to them.

"Grandma used to bring Mommy here when she was my age, and they had long talks."

"Did you have nice talks with your mother here?" the Indian man asked.

"Oh, yes," Edgar said. "She taught me all the different names for clouds and how to predict the weather before it happens."

They both laughed because outside a cloud opened with such violence that the street was suddenly filled with laughter and the excited screams of people running as if they were children.

"It's like we are in a machine being washed together," the Indian man noted.

Edgar nodded. "We used to sit where those women are," Edgar said, pointing to the women with the towels. "Mommy used to have candy in her purse, and we would buy a soda from the machine and have a sugar picnic." Edgar couldn't help but laugh as he remembered. "She told me not to tell Daddy, but one day her purse fell off the table at supper, and candy went all over the floor, and Daddy just looked at her in surprise, because there was more candy than he had probably ever seen."

The Indian man laughed, too, and then bought Edgar a soda and some candy from the machines with some of the quarters left over from lunch.

Edgar laughed so much that pieces of candy fell from his mouth, but the Indian man didn't seem to mind at all.

In the hot Laundromat, Edgar could almost smell his mother's perfumed wrists. The powder machine, with its very small but brightly colored boxes of washing powder, reminded Edgar of the small box of Joy that was on the shelf above his bed. When his mother gave him the two quarters to buy it, she had said:

"I will always give you joy"

As they left the Laundromat and walked toward the subway on Fourteenth Street, they both stopped, because there was a homeless man sleeping on a vent.

"He was once a little boy," the Indian man said sadly.

The man was covered with several blankets and lay on wet cardboard boxes. His hair was thin and ragged. His skin was coated in dirt. His shoes were three sizes too big and had no laces.

"He still is a little boy waiting for someone to love him," Edgar said.

Edgar pulled his mother's sweater from his backpack.

"What are you doing?" the Indian man asked.

"Finding a new way to love Mommy," Edgar replied.

He laid the sweater next to the man's hands, and as he did so, the cold, dirty fingers sensed the sweater's softness and reached out for it. At his feet was a badly written sign that read:

sometimes we all need help

"That was nice, what you did," the Indian man said.

"It was nothing, really," said Edgar.

"It was nothing and it was everything," said the Indian man.

"What do you mean?" asked Edgar.

"You'll see one day," he said.

A cool wind blew across the subway platform, and Edgar tried to remember what the Indian man had said, not wind, but laughter's laughter.

When the train squealed to a stop, Edgar reached for the Indian man's hand and they boarded, sitting next to a boy and his mother. The mother was peeling the shells from pistachio nuts and putting the nuts into a bag. The boy watched her, a basketball balanced on his knees.

The boy's mother was pregnant.

"All the secrets are in there," the Indian man said, pointing to her abdomen. Edgar looked at her bulging body. He had once been inside that warm house.

When they reached their stop and left the station, it was dark, and for a moment both Edgar and the Indian man were transfixed by the night sky.

"We leave one womb for another." The Indian man laughed.

Although the stars appeared to be close, they were millions of miles away.

"The light from the stars takes so long to reach us that sometimes a star will have expired by the time we can see it," the Indian man said.

"Some of these stars are dead?"

"Nothing dies in the way that we think, Edgar," the Indian man said. "Perhaps what really matters is that they are so beautiful, whether they are still awake or not."

They walked through the park, but it was so dark that even though surrounded by trees and bushes they could not see any of them. They felt only each other's presence.

As they neared Fifth Avenue, the moon crisped the tops of trees, and Edgar knew that his father was home. As they stood on the edge of Fifth Avenue, the Indian man's eyes seemed to glow and their light touched Edgar's face.

Without saying a word he adjusted his turban, turned around, and walked back into the park without once looking back. Edgar watched. The Indian man's painful amble suddenly took on a strange majesty. He seemed to grow as tall as the trees. Then his form grew bright.

Edgar looked past the avenue, past the buildings, through the clouds and into the universe.

No solid object separated him from infinity.

The sea between Edgar and his father began to drain, and in the distance burned the fire of a man waiting to be rescued by a small boy he once knew.

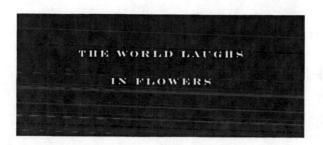

THE WORLD LAUGHS
IN FLOWERS

A few hours ago I boarded a plane at Los Angeles International Airport wearing no socks. By dawn tomorrow I shall be walking beneath the fruit trees of Athens.

Last week I received a letter from Samantha in Greece. She informed me of her forthcoming marriage to her childhood friend. We had spent only a few weeks together, five years ago, but when you finally meet the person who in daydreams you had sculpted without words, the transparency of time becomes the color of hair, and shapeless years become the shape of lips.

Perhaps we are each allotted only a certain amount of love—enough only for an initial meeting—a serendipitous clumsiness. When it leaves to find others, the difficulty begins because we are faced with our humanness, our past, our very being.

The conditions under which I left Samantha were complicated by my drinking.

I had been drinking so much back then that my skin was beginning to change color. I remember watching Samantha for the last time through the shutters as she skipped up the front steps of my apartment building, her bag swinging. I had thought I would live in Greece with her forever. But sometimes, when confronted by something of unfathomable beauty, the bars of the cage around us begin to tremble. So I ran away to protect myself and remained a prisoner.

I am somewhere above the Atlantic Ocean. I look down into the darkness and imagine a scatter of uninhabited islands. For the years Samantha and I have been apart, I have been marooned. And as if I have been stranded on one of the imaginary islands below, I am now finally drifting away on a raft tied together with thick grasses of fear and relief.

A few days after receiving Samantha's letter, I couldn't sleep and got up. I decided to go for a walk along Sunset Boulevard. It was quiet. Dawn swept through the streets. I saw a woman in a wedding dress waiting for a bus. She was slumped on a wooden bench. Her dress swam around her and across the bench, obscuring an advertisement in Spanish. Her feet hung an inch off the curb.

A veil covered her eyes. Her mouth quivered. Her lipstick looked smeared. I realized that since leaving Samantha, there was a part of me that had never stopped grieving. And all this time, it was not Samantha for whom I had often woken up sobbing, but for my self, for the plague of indifference that had kept me from her all these years. Like a ship, I had dropped anchor in the middle of the sea. I had chosen to quietly rot.

There was a man in jeans bent over beside the woman in the wedding dress. He was sifting for cans in the trash. I remember the con-

centration on his face. He was the street's unofficial archaeologist. I
thought how simple it would be for us to change places.

When suddenly I realized that I knew the woman in the wedding
dress, I decided to buy a seat on the next flight to Greece. I went home,
found my passport, and hailed a taxi for the airport.

I wonder how happy Samantha is and how many photographs have
already been taken of her and her childhood friend.

I imagine her voice.

I can see her family house, perched high above the city, its white
stone walls erupting out of scorched earth, emptying coolness into a
blue shell of sky. Her father is playing backgammon on the veranda.
His mustache is twitching. There is soccer on the television.

As the homeless man rummaged deeper into the trash for cans, the
woman in the wedding dress began to cry, and I saw through the veil
a face from long ago. But instead of rushing over and calling out her
name, I just stood there.

The woman in the wedding dress waiting for the bus is called Diane, and we lived in the same apartment building years ago. She was
training to be a nurse, and I was in my final year of a PhD in ancient
history. She lived across the hall, and we would drink chamomile tea
together. Sometimes she would discuss her knowledge of hospital pro-
cedures. Other times, I would clumsily fight my way through a passage
of ancient Greek or explain the significance of ancient bartering.

Sometimes we would hold hands for no reason or pet her cat at the
same time. I had planned to fly to Athens and write my thesis, so the
night before I moved out, we had a farewell dinner. After a long meal
with wine and the retelling of old stories, we made a promise. With my

elbows on the kitchen table, and her fingers skating across the vinyl, we agreed that if we were not married by the time we were forty, we would marry each other. Then we made love. I always wondered what happened to her. Los Angeles is a place of nightmares and fantasies.

Everyone on the airplane seems to be asleep. There are hundreds of dreams taking place around me.

I was nearing the end of my stay in Athens when I met Samantha. I had divided my time between drinking and researching the mysteries of ancient dialect for my thesis. We first kissed on the rooftop of my apartment building amid the clanking of air conditioners, below an orange sky sprayed lightly with stars. Love reveals the beauty of seemingly trivial things—a pair of shoes, an empty wine glass, an open drawer, cracks on the avenue.

I stopped drinking soon after I returned from Greece.

I stopped drinking not to prolong my life, but because abstinence allowed me to continue loving her, as though by not drinking I proved myself worthy of her companionship.

My memories are arranged like puddles—they are littered throughout the present moment. It seems arbitrary, that which the mind remembers, but I know it is not.

During the years after I left Samantha in Athens, I would often stay awake all night—not only because we were lost from one another, but because when we kissed, I had only tasted alcohol. Her childhood friend, her husband-to-be, knows how she tastes now. This is his privilege.

When the woman in the wedding dress began to cry, the homeless man who was searching for cans in the trash stood up straight and put his hand on her shoulder. Between them sat a plastic bag stuffed with crushed cans. There must have been at least two hundred. Each can had touched someone's lips.

As an archaeologist, I've often wondered how we as a race keep going through all the misery. The answer is revealed: the potential for closeness with strangers.

Floating above the mountains of the Peloponnesos, slowly descending toward Athens International Airport, saltwater caresses and soaks into the land. As passengers begin to stir, I imagine old women hanging out sheets and slicing lemons. Samantha will still be sleeping.

Outside the airport, there is a billboard advertising perfume. It shows a young, beautiful couple with the slogan: *How Does She Smell to You?*

Sleepily, I imagine the two people on the billboard are Samantha and me, and instead of taking a bus directly to Samantha's house, where her courtyard will be bursting with irises, I take a taxi in the opposite direction to the port of Piraeus. After drinking a glass of water in a café, I find the owner of a boat and pay him to take me to a small uninhabited island thirty kilometers southwest of the mainland. As we make our way out to sea, he offers me a slice of spanakopita—spinach and feta cheese pie. When Samantha made this, years ago, flour would collect on her cheeks and forehead.

As we near the island, there is a wind blowing up from the south, so I ask the captain if he can dock on a northern beach. He seems perplexed but shrugs his shoulders. When I request that he wait three hours for me, he shrugs his shoulders again and lights a cigarette. From his old radio I hear a song with the words *agapi-mou*—my love.

Slowly, I make my way to the highest point of the island. I can feel the skin on the back of my neck start to burn. I am thirsty, and sweat runs down the ridge of my back in salty corridors. I have traversed this island before. I have sipped wine amid its flowers.

I wade through purple sea daffodils and poppies. There are clusters of cyclamen, nodding—urging me to the highest point of land. I once told Samantha how the ancient Greeks referred to cyclamen as *chelonion*, because their tubers are shaped like turtles. She had kissed me and said, "The world laughs in flowers."

As I reach the pinnacle, the skin on my neck and arms begins to blister. I am as close to the sun as the island will allow, and flowers give way to dry and hollow stems of yellow. The soil has turned to bloodred dust.

As I buckle to my knees and then lay on my stomach with my chin embedded in the crimson earth, I can see a carpet of flowers lining the hillside, a gradual descent in color.

And then, as I close my eyes, the wind—after skimming along the sea, peeling its salty freshness—races up between the wildflowers, slowing as it gathers the weight of their bouquet. When the wind finally comes upon me and inhabits my shirt like ice, I inhale the memory of Samantha.

If I were to fly home without seeing Samantha, by the time my plane arrived in Los Angeles she would be married. Diane, in the wedding dress, would have boarded her bus, and the homeless man would have sold his cans.

Up here on this forgotten elbow of land, I have nothing to lose, and though I am more afraid now than I have ever been, I am relieved, I am unburdened, I am ascending.

SOME BLOOM IN DARKNESS

for Eugène Atget and Erik Satie

Since witnessing a violent incident at the railway station some months earlier, Saboné had not sketched a thing. He had not sketched the pigeons that dripped from the ledges of the Museum, nor had he shuffled through the Museum, where he liked to sit and watch people rather than paintings. Since bearing witness to the violent incident some months earlier, Saboné often became breathless with anxiety, as though he were the perpetrator of a terrible crime that he could not recall.

Saboné found a genuine pleasure in small things. He had lived with his mother in an unpretentious suburb of Paris until one day she died, and Saboné thought it best to move and make a fresh start. Since then, he had regressed into a shadow existence of adult life that seemed without beginning or end.

Over the years, he had become quite skilled at sketching things. And as he aged, Saboné realized that he was like his sketches—that it was possible to be alive and not exist at the very same moment.

The small apartment Saboné found after his mother's death overlooked a fountain. Water bubbled through the mouth of a child. Saboné's evenings were quiet, but for the crackle of a fire in winter and the sound of his fingers turning the pages of books. However, not long after his mother died, a wild and ungovernable desire grew inside him.

He hoped that by accident—perhaps on one of his long walks—he might meet a young lady of similar circumstance with whom he could spend Sunday afternoons and meet after work for large cold-platter suppers on the noisy rue du Docteur Blanche.

But this desire to meet a young lady—this sentiment, which drew him out to the cafés on the avenues—was accompanied by such an equally powerful feeling of utter insincerity that these desires, which brought welcome respite from his shadow existence, slowly migrated like a flock of rare birds.

His life went back to normal until one day after almost ten years he witnessed a violent incident at the railway station where he worked as a simple clerk. Those desires suddenly returned, and soon enough, Saboné's eyes burned for the girl who stood in a shopwindow on his walk to work. She was very pretty, and Saboné assumed he had passed her many times before on his early morning walk to the railway station, but for some reason, he had never noticed her.

In addition to this new passion for a girl, Saboné caught himself doing odd things, like talking to birds and removing his hat whenever he passed statues in the gardens.

For days, he held the image of this shopgirl in his mind, carrying it around like an egg until he could get home and escape into sleep where it hatched into a fantasy.

Without constant vigilance, Saboné slipped into daydreams. After his mother died, his daydreams began to include voices, which Saboné concluded were just overheard conversations being replayed by a decadent subconscious.

Some daydreams seemed to want to swallow him up for good. Like wild horses, they would follow him in the day and then wander the plains of his dream life, but always upon him—until he would barely remember his own name.

In his top dresser drawer, Saboné kept the sketches he thought were acceptable. He possessed two in total: one of a door with elaborate rusting hinges, and the other of a cat he had once seen peering up into the street from under a drain.

Every Friday, the girl in the shopwindow would have a new outfit and be standing in a different way.

Saboné often daydreamed while perched in his ticket box at the railway station.

"Monsieur!" the customers would cry, and Saboné would suddenly realize that it was a rainy afternoon and that he was not an Egyptian king, nor had he been sold into slavery by mistake.

The girl in the shopwindow who so preoccupied Saboné's thoughts was not really a girl because she lacked a human heart. She was made of wood. From a distance, however, she may well have been mistaken for one. And from the way she peered into the street through her glass eyes, Saboné decided that she might as well be a girl, because he believed that girls peered longingly and had secrets.

Saboné's small apartment room, where he would return each night after dispensing tickets at the station, was not big enough for two, but if she were able to come home with him, he supposed that there was certainly enough room for her to sit down quietly (if she wished to).

Saboné's face was a gray tower with a child peering from the two black windows for eyes. His was the sort of man who would suddenly stop walking and poke objects with his walking stick.

Before he began to notice the girl in the shopwindow, Saboné experienced a violent incident at the station. He had been up all night dreaming and had awakened exhausted.

All morning, through the cold glass of his ticket window at the station, Saboné was so drowsy that he had barely been able to read the schedule, to which several minor adjustments were to be made owing to expected bad weather. Instead, with dreamy irreverence, the over-tired Saboné began to sketch a woman who since buying her ticket had been sitting still not very far from his booth.

Saboné's hand glided across the paper, making the tiniest lines. Soon, they began to resemble a person, and with only a few strokes more the image began to tremble before him, as though he had tricked some part of her soul into inhabiting the picture. He admired it and then folded it several times before dropping it into the wastepaper basket as if it were the wax wrapper from some tasteless baguette.

When an arm of sunlight stretched through the glass roof of the station and engulfed her, Saboné smiled, but his mouth showed no trace of it.

At several minutes to twelve, a short, well-dressed man approached the woman, but he did not sit down. They began to chat, and Saboné wondered what the man wanted, or whether he was an old acquaintance relaying some story that had filled the void between their last meeting.

In the same way a sudden noise outside his room would release Saboné momentarily from his dreams, the short man clenched a fist and struck the woman squarely on the nose. He straightened his tie and looked as though he wanted to say something, but people were suddenly standing up, so he walked away quickly and quietly. The woman did not make a sound, but fought to control the stream of blood with a lacy handkerchief, which was soon crimson. People stared. An old man called for a gendarme.

Saboné began to shake. If he left the ticket office, the door was fixed so that he would not be able to get back in. If he asked her into the ticket box, there was a danger that someone would see and he would be dismissed—and Saboné had never been dismissed from anything, nor had he ever spoken in anger or raised his voice.

When the bleeding stopped, her eyes were swollen from crying and her nose was the color of a plum.

At fifteen minutes to one, with the handkerchief still pressed to her face, she stood up and left the station. Saboné strained to catch every last glimpse of her before she turned a corner and was gone. From the bundle she carried, she appeared to be a common girl, and Saboné wondered if she were even able to read.

Despite the demands of an old woman with an ear trumpet who wanted to know if she could leave Paris for a month but come back at the same time, Saboné reached under his desk and fished the sketch of the woman from the wastepaper basket. Without any flicker of emotion, he slipped it into his pocket as though it were evidence of the crime he had committed but had no memory of.

He explained to the old woman that she could leave on a train that departed Paris at eight minutes to two, but that it was impossible to return at the same time.

"Impossible!" she affirmed to the queue of people behind her, as though she had always suspected it.

By the time the girl in the shopwindow occupied a place in most of Saboné's daydreams, it had been two weeks since the violent incident, and the memory of it was like the memory of a dream—but it was heavier than a dream and had somehow anchored itself to Saboné. He would often think he saw her at the station. Perhaps by drawing her he had bound their shadows together—like two nights without a day between them.

When passing the girl in the shopwindow on the rue du Docteur Blanche became something Saboné looked forward to—even more so than sketching pigeons or eating supper beside the fountain—he grew afraid and found an alternative walk to the station through the city gardens. He didn't want to lose himself completely. Without her staring down at him from the window every morning and night, he could get some time to decide what to do. But Saboné began to wake at irregular hours of the night and think of her, like certain flowers in the park, flowers that will only bloom in darkness.

Saboné had one friend—a man who lived in the apartment below. His name was Oncle, and he was so large that he barely fit through the double doors of his own apartment. Saboné had never seen him venture beyond the fountain. Oncle would sob bitterly in the night as though his girth hid a swirling ocean of shame.

Saboné and Oncle exchanged cards at Christmas and often left notes for one another to acknowledge changes in the weather.

Oncle wore loose, shiny gowns and velvet carpet slippers with a gold "O" stitched on to each one. His only request in the friendship was that Saboné bring home any spare or used train tickets, which Oncle liked to arrange very prettily in cloth-covered books.

Oncle knew the train timetables by heart, and it often occurred to Saboné that Oncle would have been a far superior ticket dispenser than he if his friend were able to leave the apartment.

One wet Sunday afternoon, after a lunch of cold meat and beer, Oncle puffed on a cigar and mulled over Saboné's predicament regarding the girl in the shop. Finally, with rain upon the window like a thousand eyes, Oncle said sensibly, "Go into the shop, Saboné, and politely enquire."

The thought of entering the shop filled Saboné with such fear that, following lunch with Oncle, he immediately went to bed and was carried away by dreams, like a leaf falling from a branch into a slow river.

He awoke in the early hours of the morning, and although it was still dark, his room glowed with the soul of the snow that lay outside upon the streets and smoky roofs.

Saboné slid into his robe and crept to the window.

The courtyard and the fountain below were in a deep sleep. Saboné imagined bringing her back to his apartment. He imagined carrying her across the wedding cake snow of Paris and then her face when she saw the fountain.

The gray city was completely smothered by snow the next morning. The shop bell rang loudly as Saboné entered, kicking snow off his shoes as he went.

There were racks of dresses. There were feathered hats upon the walls like exotic birds. Inside the shop, there was no sound.

As Saboné made his way over to the window to see the girl, something appeared from between a dark rack of furs.

Saboné was not sure if it was a woman or a painted doll, but a small trembling creature suddenly appeared before him. The woman's lips were bloodred, and her skin was very white.

"Yes," the woman stated as though answering a question. She raised her cane at Saboné. "You have come to see the furs, have you?"

Coffee was brewing in the back of the shop.

"Well," she said, "do you see anything that pleases you?"

A thick paste of makeup moved when her mouth did.

"I've been noticing the girl in the window on my way to work every morning, Madame," Saboné remarked.

"I'll bet you have," the woman barked, "and you're not the first young man to politely enquire." Then breathlessly, "Reminds you of someone, does she?"

The floor of his soul creaked, as though in the silence that followed Saboné's quivering lips imparted the secrets of his loneliness, which even he did not understand.

"Who, the girl?" he said in a high-pitched voice.

They both turned to the window and watched the snow as it soundlessly found its place upon the earth.

"What is one to do?" the woman remarked. "The city gardens are quite impassable at this time of year."

"Did you know there are flowers there that bloom in darkness?" Saboné asked.

"But who goes to the gardens at night?" She snorted.

Saboné felt anger spread through his body like fire but said quietly, "I don't suppose anyone does."

As he stepped into the street, he lost his footing and jarred his head against the ledge of the shopwindow. A few spots of blood appeared in the snow. Saboné bent down in awe. His very own blood lay before him. It had been inside him for almost four decades. It had passed through his body and lubricated his dreams. The object of his desires peered coldly from the window at the few drops. He knelt down as more drops collected in the snow, and then he fingered the soft gash in his head. His forehead turned numb from the pain, and every few steps Saboné looked back at the red dots—at the eyes of his soul in the snow of the street.

When he arrived at the ticket office—late for the first time in thirteen years—the head ticket dispenser inspected him from above his spectacles. Saboné felt a line of blood warm his cheek.

"My dear boy—you've had a spill."

*   *   *

By evening, the station was almost deserted, and nearing suppertime a man approached Saboné's window and asked for a ticket to "anywhere."

"Where is that exactly?" Saboné asked.

"I can't say," the man said, without any flicker of emotion.

Saboné thought of it that night in bed.

At approximately four o'clock in the morning, Saboné sat up and went to the window. The moon was bright but expressionless. He dressed and went outside. Then he walked to the city gardens.

In moonlight, the statues moved their eyes and glowed. Saboné was not fully convinced that he was awake but wondered why he had never before swum through snow and moonlight—and why, after so many years of awkwardness, he suddenly felt as though he had found his home—and that perhaps he was a character in the dream of Paris.

Most of the plants in the garden balanced tiny burdens of snow on their tops. Although Saboné knew that it was winter and he would not see any in bloom, he realized that he had been mistaken, that it was not in darkness in which some flowers bloomed, but in moonlight.

He scooped up some of the unbroken snow and chewed it. Then he laughed. How silly he had been to fall in love with a mannequin. Silly, he thought, but understandable, considering his circumstances.

As the path widened, Saboné noticed someone sitting on a bench, and he stopped walking.

Then he recognized her and recalled the image of her bloodied handkerchief, and the spots of blood that followed her across the station to the platform—the eyes of her soul.

Her presence convinced Saboné that he must be dreaming, because she was so very white. When he got close, her eyes, which were wide open, did not follow his movement.

At last he reached out for her, but she did not move. He stroked her face with his fingers, including the nose, which, although white and free from any storm beneath, was completely frozen. Crumbs of snow that had collected in her hair were still intact.

He knelt down in the snow at her feet and remembered the sight of his very own blood outside of the shop.

He pulled himself up onto the bench. He reached around her with his arm and moved her closer. He squeezed her until he felt the bones beneath. Then he settled down and became quite still. He found the drawing of her in his jacket pocket and unfolded it. Then he put his arm around her again and wished that everyone he had ever met was somehow able to see him. It was some time before they were moved.

DISTANT SHIPS

I think of Leo very often these days. I think of him tonight as I sort packages for a truck that's headed for London. It is so cold in the warehouse that we wear our breath like beards. The office sent down a box of gloves last week, but I enjoy the feel of cardboard against my old cracked hands. I have worked for the Royal Mail for almost three decades now. I thought they would let me go when I stopped speaking twenty years ago, but they've been good to me, and when I retire in ten years I'll be given a state pension and a humble send-off. I enjoy my work. It's the only reason I leave the house, except for my walks on the beach.

Each package has somewhere to go and the contents remain a mystery. Occasionally I'll find a box where the address has been written by a child. I used to put these boxes to the side until the end of my shift so I could study the penmanship and compare it to Leo's. In a child's handwriting, language is exposed as the pained and crooked medium it really is. Since losing Leo, these packages are like shards of glass.

The warehouse is divided into sections. There are no windows, and sometimes I imagine the factory is in Oslo, Mumbai, or Rotterdam. Outside, the sopping Welsh hillsides roll away in one direction like old giants under blankets of moss. In the other direction, the land suddenly stops as though woken up. Where the land stops, something else begins, and the sea stretches north until it starts to freeze, and then it clings to the earth like a child to its mother.

Small muddy vans roll in from villages in the valleys. These vans are unloaded and the packages sorted by nearest city. Every two days, hulking lorries chug from the warehouse to Glasgow, Manchester, London, and Penzance.

As I walk home each morning in the dark, I picture headlights carving through night's flesh. I love the names of the towns on the packages the same way I love the different species of weeds that blindly push through the shell of earth around the forked gate of my house.

Hundreds of years ago, the village relied solely on fishing. I have a book of paintings in my sitting room at home. One of the paintings has young women in aprons standing on cliffs watching a ship get smashed against the rocks. In the foreground is an arm of sunlight reaching down to the surface of the sea. I couldn't tell you who painted the picture, but I understand the inclusion of that long beam of light, I understand the grief that makes such details necessary. There is little fishing work in this town now.

Although the warehouse provides more of a steady income than fishing, all the boys in the village dream of going to sea. They dream with their windows open of ancestors on the sorts of ships you only see in bottles now.

Sometimes I walk along the rocky beach beneath the village. The dark green water sweeps in, and I scream with the roar of dragging rocks. I spend hours peering into rock pools at fish and crabs. I wonder if they know they've been cut off. I like to sit on the cold pebbles until the tide sloshes over my shoes and water soaks through my socks and pulls at my toes like some hysterical being.

When early morning comes and my shift ends, I write down the number of vans that I unloaded. After thirty years, I've never made a mistake, because for me, each truck is like a person. As a boy I always felt that vehicles had faces.

I clock out and find my coat in the break room. There is a half-eaten sandwich on the table. A calendar of topless women hangs from one of the lockers. The women look cold. They wear large smiles. Perhaps photographs can fake happiness, but never grief.

The warehouse is half an hour's walk from the village, first through a narrow country lane and then up a hill into town past hedgerows thick with birds peering out from their nests. In summer, wild berries replace the black eyes of the birds.

In a few hours dawn will flood the world. I stop walking and lean against a lamppost. My left leg always hurts, and it's worse in winter. Everything is worse around Christmas.

The light from the streetlamp falls upon my hands. They are the color of stained glass. In the village church there is a magnificent stained-glass window. Sometimes I kneel beneath it and drown in color. When the pain in my leg is back to a dull throbbing I continue walking. Stones caught in the tracks of my boots scrape the concrete. I miss autumn—the season when summer takes on the memory of its own mortality. And then winter. And then the miracle season, when everything begins again fearlessly.

The walk home is always slow, and rows of slate houses glisten. Their black foreheads are white with tomorrow's breath. Curtains are pulled across the eyes from within.

A bird hops around a lamppost. There is a plump worm in its beak. It flies away as I approach.

I pass the corner pub. Even though it's against the law, pubs in the village are open all the time on account of the few remaining fishermen who return an hour or so before dawn, with a thirst built up from being on the water without being able to drink any of it. The light spills out into the street with the sound of laughing. I smell beer, and a dull thud from the jukebox reminds me of my leg, which reminds me of Leo.

A mist wraps around the town. Its white arms spread through the streets. Dogs bark at kitchen doors.

I used to go into the pub for a pint or two. But I haven't been in for about six years. It's all so useless.

After Jeanne took Leo's things to America twenty years ago, I felt a sense of relief. The house was quiet, and for some reason I began to think about my mother, who died when she was sixty-eight. The same year Jeanne and I were married. My mother slipped on some ice and broke her hip, then without any warning she died in the hospital. It was like the closing of a book I never thought could end.

I spent last Sunday watching the fishing boats chug home, their hulls thick with silver pellets of fish.

I haven't said a word in twenty years, but there was a time when you wouldn't have been able to shut me up. I've lived so long without the pain of language. My life is a letter with no address.

If you were to watch me for an afternoon, you'd notice that my hands are always moving. Like blind siblings they are always touching one another.

I like watching the fishing boats. Each boat's arrival is celebrated by a spray of birds. Seagulls from a distance look like eyes drifting over the waves. Last week one of the young captains asked if I needed work. I shook my head. He was a handsome boy, probably about the age Leo could have been. I wonder who has inherited the life Leo left behind.

I live in the house I grew up in. My parents' room is the same. It is the guest room, but the only guests are ghosts who drift in through the doorways in dreams.

Everybody in the village knows my life story. But I'm too old to think my sadness is special.

Jeanne is my age, but lives a different life. In this village with its damp shoes and Sunday hymns, you are old the moment someone you love dies. And then Sundays are spent watching light move across the garden from small hot rooms that smell like ironing.

Jeanne lives in Los Angeles. We're still married, though we haven't spoken since Leo. I think they make pictures in Los Angeles. Perhaps her life is a long fantasy.

Sometimes I linger outside the junior school at the bottom of the hill. At this time of year, Christmas decorations hang in the windows. Beyond the school are mountains dotted with sheep and the odd light of a tractor grinding its way home. Sometimes I time my walks to co-incide with the three o'clock school bell. Children gush into the play-ground like hot water and into the arms of their parents. I would give everything, even memory—especially memory—if I could hold Leo again. The weight of his absence is the weight of the entire world.

I stopped speaking soon after the accident in the hope I'd retain the memory of his soft, lispy voice. Sometimes I cup one of Leo's words in my hands like a trembling bird. After the accident, the doctors said I had only a few months to live. Jeanne went back to America, and I waited for that journey home. I felt like packing a suitcase but didn't know what to put in it. That was twenty years ago. I have stopped go-ing to doctors. They only believe what they think they know. They are like priests—blinded from spirituality by religion.

Jeanne would be shocked if she could see how bleak everything is, though the village hasn't really changed, except for cars being allowed in the marketplace and a link road through the mountains for lorries. When I thought I was going to die after the accident, I started writing a book, and then never stopped writing. It is called *Dreams Are Lost Cities of Childhood.*

I have worked on it every day for twenty years. I will not be finished until I'm dead. The book I'm writing is the book to end all books. My death will be the concluding chapter. I have drawn all the pictures, too. The book is about my life with Leo and Jeanne. I cannot draw my-self, so I mark my body in the pictures with an X. Sometimes when I read old chapters, I am suddenly in the midst of how things were—it's like being on a theater set that someone has built of your life. Memory is like life but with actors.

Jeanne wakes up to sunshine. She drinks orange juice. Los Angeles is warm, even at this time of year. Leo would be a man now. Some people have Christmas at the beach in America. They do in Australia, too. I wake to rain tapping on the window like a hundred Welsh mothers. Each drop is a note on the minor scale.

Jeanne came here to study the climate. There is a university in Bangor. Students come from across the world to watch clouds. I remember watching her marvel at the slow, swirling explosions of white. I offered her a paper cup of cockles. That was when you could buy them from a cart, but it's long since gone. It was where old people met and talked about the war. Jeanne's accent was smooth and rich. I used to wish that my ancestors had gone to America. Perhaps then things would have been different. Perhaps we could have met at the cinema, a drive-in. Perhaps Leo and I would have worked on an old car together—the sort people build in their garages.

Twenty years ago, I drove off the side of a cliff. I was trying to make Leo laugh by turning around to make faces. It's as simple as that.

Leo's body was recovered half a mile from the wreckage. He looked as though he were asleep, but his insides were liquid. I like to think he was carried from the car by the same angels that drift in and out of the stories I've grown fond of reading by Milton and Blake. They wrote beneath the same moon that's above the village. Everything that's ever happened, the moon saw.

They tell me I survived the accident.

It's Wednesday morning. Darkness at this hour is seldom remembered. Most people are about to wake up. I stand lopsided outside my front door. It is not really a door, but another gateway to sadness. It begins to drizzle. The fog rolls away and creeps up the black hillside. Fires are being lit. Mornings in Wales reek of frying eggs and wood smoke. Children are stirring in warm beds. Soon they will be released from the arms of dreams. All arms are envoys of God. It is night here, but day somewhere else, and somehow it keeps going and going whether we're a part of it or not.

Suddenly the sky is full of rain; drops the size of thumbs. It will soon be Christmas. The children at school are putting on a play. They make their own costumes. Night is a tattered veil suspended. The moon is full and absent all at once. Leo's face waits for me in every mirror. Dreams are the unfinished wings of our souls.

NO GREATER GIFT

Way above the Park, traffic has stopped. A fat woman in tight clothes pushes twins in a stroller. The eyeballs of the twins slide up to the elevated train. The train grieves into the station.

Gabriel watches the twins and then looks into the space they are being pushed. Gabriel looks down at his watch and shuffles into an alley behind a bakery. His package should be ready.

A steel door opens separating a word sprayed in white. Two trembling hands emerge holding a box tied with string. There is a bird tattooed on one of the hands. Gabriel places his hands on the top and bottom and only when the other hands feel the responsibility of weight transfer do they release and disappear back behind the steel door. Gabriel taps twice and looks around.

As Gabriel makes his way through the alley toward the subway, he pauses beside a motorcycle lying on its side. He is tempted to open the box for a quick peek at what's inside.

Two men waiting for the train look Gabriel over. Their pants are baggy and remind Gabriel of sails. Their eyes want to know what he is carrying and why he is handling it with such care. They look at the hole in Gabriel's sneakers. They look at Gabriel's scar. He was in a fire. There were several deaths. It crosses his cheek and disappears under his ear. People notice it because it is a lighter shade of brown than the rest of his face. His mouth hangs open, a habit that makes him look absent but that his wife loves.

As he stares down the track into the light of an approaching train, he considers what he is doing and thinks about his mother. The train brings with it a cold wind that makes the two men on the platform forget about Gabriel.

The silver doors slide open. An intercom spits out a muffled message. The subway car is full of short Mexican men with paint on their sneakers. They are huddled together but don't talk. One of them is reading a tattered children's book to improve his English. Gabriel notices a boy and a girl, perhaps seven or eight years old. Their grandfather—a mustache curling down each side of his chin—is asleep with his mouth open. The boy is amused by this. The Mexican man reading the children's book is concentrating so hard that he doesn't notice the girl lean and mouth the words as he thinks them.

The train crosses an unmarked boundary into Brooklyn. Gabriel looks at the other passengers, but only an old woman in black is watching him. As he looks at her, her eyes fall on to the box and then she turns her body away from Gabriel toward the glass of the door. Gabriel's mother once told him that if you keep thinking of someone dead, you summon them.

As the train rushes into light and slows, Gabriel is able to see the people who might step into his car. He notices a transit cop. The transit cop doesn't move from the platform, then is lost behind the rush of men in suits and women in long coats with long hair. He moves the box onto his lap and rests it on his thighs. As he pulls the bottom of his coat over it, he realizes how dirty he must look, because his sneaker has a hole in it and his coat is stained black in places. He looks at how clean the new passengers are and remembers the smell of freshly ironed shirts on Sunday nights. He hasn't worn a shirt like that since his wedding. His mother was still alive then and made paper butterflies to put in his bride's hair.

The people standing around Gabriel do so uncomfortably. He is hiding something, and they know it. He wants to stand and offer his seat, but the package must be delivered intact. When Gabriel coughs, people bury their heads. His wife wants him to see a doctor, but doctors cost money, he tells her.

A woman with short black hair in a pink raincoat is laughing to herself. The woman reminds Gabriel of his sister who lives in a suburb of Havana. She is always depressed because the man she loves is a drunk.

Gabriel is being watched by tourists. He knows they are not from the city because they are each holding a map and the women have hair that is neither fashionably styled nor untidy. They are huddled together like the Mexican men next to them. The women chatter and the men stare coldly at the floor and at the bulge under Gabriel's coat.

The car is continually full, because when people alight, others are there to take their place. Gabriel wonders how many people occupy one seat in a day, and if the seat could record the thoughts of the occupants, what it would say about human beings.

Another stop and a young blind man is helped onto the train by a girl with bleached hair. She tenderly applies pressure to his elbow. A suit immediately rises and the young blind man sits, nodding gratefully for each gesture. Everybody looks at the blind man because he cannot look back at them. He knows people are watching him and sits very still, only once adjusting his white stick so it's propped against his thigh.

Gabriel closes his eyes and imagines being blind. He feels the box below him in the darkness and grips it tightly, making sure it is still only a bulge under his coat. When he opens his eyes the train is not moving and the blind man has vanished. The doors are open. It is his stop. Gabriel rushes between the bodies stepping into the car. He repositions the box under his coat and then walks toward a stairway at the end of the platform.

Leaning against a steel girder, Gabriel peers down at the tracks. Only last week someone jumped.

There is a Chinese woman playing a bamboo flute. It is cold but she is barefoot. Tied around her neck is a pink scarf. Gabriel listens to each note. It is a very slow song, which Gabriel thinks is somehow related to the pink scarf. She has no box or hat to collect money. He lays a quarter next to her foot.

Gabriel steps into the empty car of a new train and sits below an advertisement for laser eye-surgery. He carefully raises the box to his nose and sniffs. From the smell, he tries to conjure a picture of what could be inside and what his wife will think.

Gabriel stands up and looks into a neighboring car. He can see a homeless woman with her head slumped over. She is holding a shoe and crying. Gabriel cannot make out her features because the glass in the door has been written on.

Gabriel thinks about the photograph of his sister from Havana taken at Coney Island when she came to visit. She has her arm around Gabriel's wife. It is Gabriel's favorite photograph because it is how he dreamed life would be when he was a child.

He remembers how they had laughed and eaten hot dogs with ketchup dripping off the ends.

Gabriel alights and then waits for the train to disappear into darkness before making his way aboveground. On the yellow strip that separates the platform and the track there are broken crack vials. Gabriel tries to conceal the box with even greater effort.

His footsteps echo as he makes his way on to the cold street. As he passes a gas station, he can see two fat men watching soccer on TV and smoking. Farther along he passes a man yelling into a pay phone and notices that the receiver is not connected.

The houses here have white bars dividing the glass and the street, but through the bars Gabriel can see people eating, watching TV, and arguing. In one apartment there is a boy sitting alone eating an orange.

Gabriel turns down a street, which used to be a row of crack houses. But they've been bought and will soon be demolished. He comes upon an old factory building. With trembling fingers he pulls out a key from his pocket and pushes it into a thick steel door. He steps over an empty suitcase and begins the climb to the top floor.

His hands are shaking so much that he is worried about damaging the contents of the box. He reassures himself that it will be soon be out of his hands. When he reaches the top, he stares out through a glassless window at Manhattan. The Empire State Building is shrouded in mist. Perhaps one day it will be on display as an ancient obelisk. From below the window a woman screams once.

Gabriel knocks seven times on the door and then slides keys into several locks. He pushes on the door and slips inside. At one end of the room is the faint glow of a television. Beside a sunken couch is a bed covered in mostly broken toys.

Asleep on the couch is a boy just turned three. Gabriel kneels before him as his wife emerges from behind a curtain.

"José sneak it out the back like he say?" his wife asks. Gabriel nods.

The light from the TV flickers across the boy's face. Gabriel touches the boy's knee and then shakily unties the string of the box. As the boy rubs his eyes and sits up, Gabriel presents the box to the boy and opens the lid.

"Surprise!" Gabriel and his wife say.

The boy stares at the cake—the skillfully written number three—the thick icing that rounds the cake like a crown and the cream that lazes from the middle. The boy doesn't touch the cake but covers his face with his hands and peeks at it from behind his small fingers.

SNOW FALLS AND THEN DISAPPEARS

My wife is deaf. Once she asked me if snow made a sound when it fell and I lied. We have been married twelve years today, and I am leaving her.

She is in the bakery on the corner where it is warm and they know her. She will return within an hour to our apartment with a box full of little cakes ordered especially for this day. She will return home and toss her keys into the ceramic ashtray. She will place the cakes in the fridge, where she likes to keep canned goods. She will curse my tardiness. After several hours of my absence she will develop a further deafness.

There is a very small tear in the couch I never noticed until now; a piece of leather hangs off like a tongue. It is a small rip but has ruined the entire couch and thrown the apartment into disarray. The ashtray is empty and tempts me to smoke again. My lungs are hollow and long for the return of weight.

She plays the violin every day, and I am taking it with me. It was made in 1783 in Prague. My bag and the violin sit on the bed, poised for exile. The violin goes out of tune whenever it enters a new environment, as though it loses confidence before a performance. She told me that in the darkness of its body, swimming between the maple ridges, there is a piece of her living secretly, fed by scherzo and allegro. I am taking the violin for this reason. The violin leans against my bag on the bed. Inside, quiet as dust, a part of my wife awaits resurrection.

I have a habit of lying awake between dreams, when there is no traffic and it is very cold outside, so cold that a rough white skin forms across houses and cars. I lie next to her and imagine the vibration of pumping blood reverberating through her ears; a countdown to irremediable deafness.

She is watching the fat baker squeeze icing in the shape of our proverbial hearts onto little cakes that we are supposed to share with our shallow friends tomorrow night. She is not shallow, but deaf and ungovernable. She once told me that she loved me because I was the only thing she could hear. She can feel the vibration of the strings through the carved vessel of her instrument, but I am inside her. I am a song soaked into each bone of her secret body where the world has not been able to wander.

The baker is packing up the cakes into a pink box that he will tie with a pink ribbon. The baker knows her by name and has a tight pad of paper and a pen to write down the cost of her bundle and express his gratitude. I want to leave before she leaves the bakery, otherwise I will be caught and have to wait another year. I have to be on my way to the airport with her violin and my clothes before her keys leave her hand for the ceramic ashtray.

I have already burned all the photographs; they made a crackle and set off the smoke detector, which I promptly smashed. She won't need it because she is deaf and it gives off only a minute vibration.

I am taking one of her favorite dresses, which I know is a mistake. I remember falling asleep as she laid it out among the tendrils of to-morrow. The dress was a bridge between today and tomorrow. And then together we drifted helplessly into sleep—ice melting through cracks in the floor.

I have written down all the reasons why I am leaving, though I am overcome with a sad strength for the world because I have not spoken to anyone all day. My resignation to being alone is a sea under which I can breathe.

We met in Minnesota, in the lobby of a Days Inn right off the high-way. I sat opposite her. When a waiter brought her a tray of coffee, I realized she was deaf and could not hear the cups singing. Their song made me think of my mother, wheeling herself around the kitchen, gliding through steam from the pots and pans on the stove. Many years later when she passed on and I sold her house I noticed the grooves of her chair in the linoleum floor; it was a Braille only I understood—a mother's geometry.

I am booked on an airplane to Minnesota, where I will rent a car and arrive at the hotel where we first met. There I will sit in the same seat and read the same passage in the same book. There I will wait for her to find me again, so we can step into the direction we left behind and forgot about. It is a canvas unpainted by memory.

My mother was disabled because she was shot in the legs by a Nazi officer in Berlin. In reaction to the linoleum floor forty years later, I wrote a book about her and by accident found a picture of the officer who shot her. His name was Hans.

I have recently hung a blanket across the bathroom window and unscrewed the lightbulb. This was a strange operation induced by the sight of my wife's toothbrush, which sat bolt upright in a chrome stand. Whenever I washed my hands or bathed, the toothbrush would stare silently at me, challenging my faltering courage.

When a person disappears one day on her walk home from a bakery, the toothbrush becomes a symbol of hope.

I would wake in the night to feel its bristles, to check for wetness. If I am able to see its yellow spine, I'll have to wait another year. I picture the bakery and the cakes; I can smell the butter and taste each hot mouthful.

The Nazi soldier who disabled my mother was called Hans, he was my father, and they were lovers. That is why she lived and made it to America, because I was inside her. I was her protector, a tiny forbidden inception. I have a picture of him, which I never showed my wife, because she might not have understood why I am proud. I have inherited his stoicism. I have inherited his ability to love. We are united through loss.

The square clapped and crackled with gunfire. Heads fell against wet cobbles. People were separated from their shoes.

My father. His eyes shut. Dispatching round after round into men, women, and children. And then reason suddenly gripping him. He opens his eyes quickly enough to lower his gun.

Although my father snapped the bullets into my mother, I like to think it was his love for her that instinctively deflected them away from her heart.

As people became bodies, indistinguishable from one another, my father scooped up my mother. He took her to the Jewish ghetto and found a doctor whose family was starving. The doctor stopped the bleeding and removed the bullets of my father's pistol without asking for so much as an apple. Before I imagined deafness, I would lie awake thinking of my mother on the train hurtling across frozen Germany—the mountains dotted with soldiers in heavy coats, smoking and thinking of their wives. I could picture the border guards perusing her papers and wheeling her onto a cold platform, where freight trains stuffed with meat and fruit and wine would trundle lugubriously before people whose stomachs were paralyzed with hunger. My mother had a photo of her mother's flower garden tucked down her dress that separated me from a torn continent.

It snowed the morning she left Liverpool for New York. That's how I knew that I would marry the woman drinking coffee—when she asked me if snow made a sound when it fell. She wrote this question on the palm of her hand.

There are some lies that, under the right circumstances, are the only truth.

We slept naked that night in the hotel, a bundle of limbs, an arrangement of muscle and bone held together by fear and newness.

Although I knew she would have invited the waiter up to her room had he been sitting where I was and looking at her as I was, I didn't care. I wanted to stretch into the ridge of her spine and complete her back, as water freezes in the crevice of a rock. The next morning it was snowing, and she asked me. I thought of my mother and said, "Yes." I wanted to carry her deafness away from the restaurant and lay its marvel in the snow. That night I went to her performance. She played Bach's Concertos in A Minor and E Major for Violin, and I pictured my mother changing her name at Ellis Island and then making her way to my birthplace.

I learned my wife's sign language. "Ballet for Fingers" we called it. We never spent one day apart until she disappeared walking home with a box of cakes. I wonder what happened to the cakes, were they ever eaten? By whom? The cakes torture me. And now the bakery is open again, its lights spilling out on to the cold street below the windows of children's bedrooms.

My father was killed by a seventeen-year-old Polish partisan in the fall of 1943. He was younger than I am now. My mother never spoke much of Europe, though I could picture it through her stories of her father, who sold bicycles until his shop was closed down. Once, I brought a friend home from school. He was born in Switzerland and spoke fluent German. I remember presenting him to her, and as his mouth pressed into the language, my mother began to cry and the boy stopped what he had only just begun.

Sometimes, language is the sound of longing. The small Boeing will be my ship from Liverpool. The violin will be my exit papers.

As the elevator slows to the level of the lobby, the doors separate to reveal a frail Russian named Eda who has lived in the building for sixty years. She puts her hand on my sleeve and looks concerned. She wants to know how I've been coping and where I am going with the violin. She wants to know if, after so long, there has been some news. I tell her that my wife is in the bakery buying cakes iced with proverbial hearts, and I have to be in the car heading for the airport before she returns. I tell her it is our anniversary and I am leaving her. This makes her cry and she lets me go, giving me strength—the strength of my father as he carried my mother through the freezing rain, along cobbled streets, between tall dank houses scarred with lines of bullet holes, pushing his way through the nightmare, his face streaked with blood, his heart burning with disgrace. I can picture them clinging to one another, though lost from each other forever. I can see his face as the Jewish doctor feverishly looks for the bullets. I can imagine the night she left and the emptiness that followed him. I imagine his memory of my mother, her falling torso, the smell of her wet hair, the trail of blood through the ghetto, the falling of snow.

THE SHEPHERD
ON THE ROCK

I have always been attracted to the idea of heaven, and that's why John F. Kennedy International Airport seemed like a good place to live out the last of my life.

You can tell who travels often because they have a convenient pocket or special wallet for their passport. The less-traveled forage for their documents, then drag their luggage into the rectangle made up of lines. Every time the line moves, another person joins.

I imagine I am watching the dead ready themselves for ascension into His kingdom, and though I no longer believe in God, the idea of a heaven and hell seems to me quite useful ways of rewarding the good and punishing the bad while they're still alive.

I'm homeless because I suffer from a madness I am too ashamed to bear responsibly. When I am momentarily free from these terrible feelings, I spend whole days and nights at the airport, sometimes sitting in a plastic chair for several hours and at other times ambling around the food court. When the terrible feelings return and from the base of my spine they stretch through my body like ghosts, I slip away from the terminal and find refuge in a shipping yard where floodlights ensure that day never completely ends.

When the madness comes I wrap myself in blankets and squeeze into this small space under one of the giant rusting containers where I know I'll be safe. Underneath, I watch the rust spread across the metal like a slow tide of autumn.

An attack begins with amnesia. I suddenly forget things, such as what I've eaten for breakfast (if anything) or when I last smoked a cigarette. Then my limbs begin to tremble slightly and my teeth knock (imagine the chattering of plates in a kitchen cabinet moments before an earthquake).

The violent shaking often lasts for several hours, but that's not the worst of it, because the ghosts trapped in my body have found a small door that leads into my memories, and so for two days and nights, I am taken blindfolded down a path into myself and forced to relive random scenes from my life. Imagine that, forced into your self.

On the morning of the first day of madness, I may be swimming with my father in a cold pond as my mother looks on breathlessly, her apron flapping in the wind like a white wing; then by afternoon I am back at the seminary in Dublin being handed my degree as my hand is shaken vigorously by the cardinal.

I hide myself now so as not to hurt anyone. When the madness passes like a child's night of terror, I wake up and can barely walk from thirst—I also defecate in my clothes, which is unpleasant, but there's a homeless shelter two hours' walk from the container yard, and so I'm able to wash my clothes and take a hot shower. A young woman from

Puerto Rico who works at the shelter always gives me a little money and a good meal. She sits down with me sometimes and says, "Whenever you're ready for a change, Paddy—just tell us." She calls me Paddy because I'm Irish and she doesn't know my real name. She often tells about her life, without asking anything about mine. I like it like that because I wouldn't want to tell her that I used to be a priest because she wears a gold crucifix—faith is a balancing act.

If there really is a God (I'm not saying there isn't—I'm just saying that I don't believe in Him, like a mother who's given up on her son's delinquent ways), I hope He helps her find the love of her life as she's a decent girl and deserves more than a string of no-good boyfriends. I've seen a few young men at the airport who I thought might be good for her, but you never know if they're coming back. Anyway, I pray for her as I walk briskly back to the airport all fresh and without that terrible stench coming from down below. I can sometimes go two full weeks without an attack, but I exist utterly in its shadow.

It was my mother's idea that I become a priest, but it was my love for people that convinced me she was right. My seminary friends and I never spent evenings at the pub or courting girls on benches by the river Liffey like other students in Dublin at the time. We'd sit around listening to the wireless with tea and toast, or on nights when a heavy rain or the quiet drama of snowfall caused a stir, we'd talk about a love for God and the many incomprehensible sides of His character.

I was a great reader and listener of music. I remember having great admiration for Voltaire, whose belief in God seemed quite secondary to his compassion. He said, "If God did not exist, it would be necessary to invent him." I agree completely. A short time after leaving the priesthood I was feeding pigeons in the park when I met the woman who would become my wife.

That was long ago. I now live at the airport. I know all the different terminals and have spent so much time staring at the Arrival and Departure boards that I could tell you when the next plane is leaving for anywhere.

It's always nice to know an airplane has been somewhere and is back safe—you can tell this by the flight numbers. When I watch people line up at the check-in desks, I sometimes try and make eye contact with children so when I pray to allay their fears, I can see the pools of their eyes and then drop my prayers into them like coins being dropped into a well.

You might say that praying is useless if I don't believe in God anymore, but let me tell you my opinion: praying for someone is a way to love them without ever having to know them.

I pity anyone who knows me, because after the trembling—when the ghosts howl at my blood and twist their ethereal limbs about my bone—I'm not myself. I once killed a dog. It was a terrible mess, and I cried for days about the dog's soul.

The ghosts always find out where I'm hiding and escort me onto the stage of my childhood. The ghosts wait in the wings as characters from my past begin to appear upon the stage. My lines are already written and cannot change; my role is the same and the only member of the audience is my self.

I try not to talk to anyone at the airport (because they'll want to know about me, and keeping things from people is a form of deception), but I'm a chatterbox at heart and sometimes get roped into a discussion with a passenger as he or she waits to be called to ascension; this is one thing we have in common.

I remember a nice story that a young pregnant lady told me about how she met her husband. I don't remember much of what she said, but I remember thinking that inside her belly was the complete soul of an unknown in a vessel the size of a bread loaf. I've often wondered at what moment the soul inhabits the cells. I suppose it's like a light that gets switched on when everything is in place. But don't ask me who switches it on, because I wouldn't like to say.

I do enjoy watching people disappear through the doors into a sun-drenched corridor.

On the door it says: TICKETED PASSENGERS ONLY.

Imagine there were a heaven and getting to it were this easy. You just received your tickets in the mail, and then after several identity checks and a few extra charges, you were on your way.

The damned would have to remain on earth in perpetual doubt.

Once an airplane swings up into the clouds, it may as well be on its way to some celestial paradise. It's hard for people to say good-bye to their loved ones. I remember an Indian man who went through the doors with several plastic bags of clothes. His children wouldn't stop crying, and once he'd gone, those he'd left behind strained to see through tiny windows for one last glimpse. This happens often, and on one occasion there were so many people trying to catch glimpses of their loved ones, an airport employee had to intervene.

You may wonder why I haven't killed myself because living with madness or watching it flood the heart of someone we love is unbearable. Don't think I haven't considered it. If I were to do it, it would be when the amnesia starts, before the trembling. I would go to the ship-ping yard, climb up the side of an oil drum, and toss my body from it. I wouldn't mind a nice burial—with a service, so I'd probably try and find a dog dollar and then the powers that be might feel compelled to do the honors—how would they know I'd lost my faith?

Back in Dublin as a young man, I was obsessed with a song by Franz Schubert called "The Shepherd on the Rock"—you may have heard of it. I would lie down on the covers of my bed and, half asleep, put the record on, then watch the last of the day drain from my room. The song is about a shepherd who lives in the mountains with his flock. Apart from his sheep, he is completely alone. He dreams of a love far away (I always imagined a distant, flickering village), and then he starts to feel terribly depressed. Just when it seems as if he can't go on, some-thing happens in the song—a slow unraveling of hope and beauty spreads throughout his rocky province and he is suddenly filled with inexplicable joy. I've planned my death so many times, but then, as I'm drifting through an empty terminal like wind, or reading a forgot-ten magazine in the restroom, I feel a strange sensation, a sense of hap-piness, and I remember my son and wife.

If only the terrible ghosts would take me to the park on Sunday so I could kick a ball around with my boy like I used to, or sit me back in the hot kitchen with a towel around my shoulders, as my wife set about giving me a haircut.

If there is a heaven, I wonder whether I'll see them there and whether my madness will remain on earth, like clothes shed before a swim.

A family once sat beside me in the terminal. I shall never forget it.

They were en route to London from Minnesota. Only the father had left the country before. There were three of them in total: a father, a mother, and a son.

The boy was in his thirties and wore a special padded head restraint. His face was contorted with an expression of pain, and his clawlike hands were pressed tightly to his chest. His eyes were neither jittery nor vicious, but slow, soft green hillsides upon which he had been trapped for decades.

We couldn't stop looking at one another, and when his bony limbs erupted in spasms, his mother said, "He has something to tell you— there's something he's trying to say to you."

Like the shepherd from his rock, I thought.

I wonder if in heaven his fingers will uncoil and reach out for his mother's soft curls. I wonder if he'll take his father for walks through clouds with pocketfuls of words. I still think about that man and sometimes dream of him naked and beautiful beneath the earth in a dark, slippery cave trying to feel his way into the light.

Two Sundays ago I passed a church that looked like the one where I used to give Mass, and I had something of an epiphany. I realized that it wasn't God, the Devil, or death that terrified me—but the fact that everything continues on after, as though we'd never existed. I sat on the steps and listened to the singing inside, to the strength of many voices singing as one. Birds swooped down to snatch scraps of food off the roadside.

Last night, I spent the evening watching snow fall onto the runway from a quiet corner of the terminal.

Different-sized trucks were deployed, and they circled the tarmac like characters in a mechanical ballet. As the flakes thickened and lay still, I wondered if my wife could see me from beyond and how ashamed I would be if she could.

And if the snow were never cleared off the runway, it wouldn't matter, because it would one day disappear of its own accord; then one day return, perhaps accompanied by wind, or by stillness, or by the sound of breathless children pulling sleds.

EVERYTHING IS A
BEAUTIFUL TRICK

I am standing along my road. It is early evening, and each house is tucked back into a pocket of vegetation. The only cars are stationary and barely visible through low branches, which hover over the houses and cars like hands.

My wife naps back at our old wooden house—a house so tired its limbs creak as though it is speaking back to the weight of our random movements.

I cannot walk farther because something sweeps through me—something so sad it renders the world broken and perfect all in the same feeling. I can tell that someone very close to me has died—that Magda has been taken away.

My wife was jealous of Magda for many years, even though they had never met.

I have stopped walking beside a house several houses down from my own. There is an old car in the front yard, its doors heavy and tires flat. A skin of pollen has gathered across the windows. The vinyl roof has peeled and flaps in the wind; the promise of a storm.

The windshield wipers are frozen in place halfway across the glass. Coated in pollen, they resemble two arms reaching out from under the hood. Ghosts kiss in the backseat. Memories spill out through a cracked window, melt into the ground between tall grass, and are pushed back up as wildflowers. Somewhere along the street a screen door yawns.

The feeling that Magda is lost fills me, swelling the skin of memory like a balloon being inflated.

Above the car there is a grocery bag caught on a branch stealing mouthfuls of wind.

My father adopted Magda from Poland, from Kraków when I was seven. My mother had left by then. Magda didn't know her at all. Magda was a long girl with short, unevenly chopped hair. Her left arm was missing at the elbow.

We shared the attic at our small house in Cornwall. We would wake early on Sunday mornings and make breakfast for my father, who would be out surfing. Even in winter, he would paddle through the freezing fog into deeper water.

Some mornings, the sky was so dark and the wind so fierce we would light candles and pretend we lived in a cave.

My father began surfing in storms after my mother decided one day that she wanted to live in Australia with her boss and his children. I was two. I barely remember her, but I am still in love with her ghost.

After setting out a brick of bread and a nest of boiled eggs, Magda and I would keep watch from the staircase, and when we saw the lights of his old Land Rover bouncing up the muddy driveway, we would skip down and open the door. This became a weekend ritual. When he stepped into the warm kitchen, he would laugh at the candles and rub my head with his salty hand. He would give Magda his wet suit, and she would drag it into the bathroom with her only hand, leaving a trail of sand and seawater on the carpet.

Over breakfast he would tell us about the sea and if anything had been washed up. Once, an American airplane from World War II tumbled onto the rocky beach after a terrific storm. My father took us to see it after breakfast. The rain was so fierce that Magda and I shared a garbage bag with holes cut for our heads. We were amazed by the fuselage of the airplane, which lay on its side. Two barrels of a machine gun poked out of a glassed dome. My father said its wings probably broke off when it hit the water. He said they'd probably not be long in coming if the tide was right. Magda and I wanted to go inside, but my father said no in a voice that meant no bargaining. Magda suggested we say a prayer to the sea, and my father said he couldn't have hoped for a more sensitive daughter. That was one of the best mornings of my life.

As my father told us stories over hot bread and eggs, seawater would sometimes drip from his nose.

When Magda first arrived from Poland and could only communicate with her eyes, we would take long walks together through the village and always stop at the same place to sit and watch old people lawn bowl. Later, when she could speak English, she told me her name for the bench beside the bowling green—*niebo*. Heaven.

On summer nights when the lingering light blushed and then disappeared, I often mused on how objects kept up with us. How lucky, what magical synchronicity, that soulless things should not only occupy the instant, but travel through time with us at the same speed, as though everything were perched high on the crest of a wave surging forward into the unwritten.

Later, on that same bench before the bowling green, when we were both eighteen years old, I told Magda about the mystery of soulless things keeping up with us, moving through time at the same speed. She laughed intelligently and told me that sometimes it is we who get left behind, anchored to memory. That is why she said she liked watching the old people in white play bowls, because they had slipped from time and hovered above the past.

We were on the verge of separation.

As we sat on the bench, as we often had for twelve years, I knew something was being taken from us. We were on the boundary of adulthood: I was leaving for America—a surfing scholarship to a college in California—and she to a prestigious university in Warsaw.

I still imagine Poland through descriptions in her letters she wrote from her university—storks nestling on rooftops, the grassy, minty dullness of marjoram, and the heavy pungency of caraway blowing through the Carpathian Mountains.

It was in silence on the bench beside the bowling green that I knew I would never see Magda again, or that if I did, we would have evolved beyond reconciliation. Without words, we mutually allowed experience to swallow us whole. It was the only way forward. But her absence would haunt me in the same way my mother's absence haunted my father, and the missing part of Magda's arm haunted her.

Now that I'm married and living in California with my wife, I think living with the absence of someone we love is like living in front of a mountain from which a person—a speck in the distance, on some distant ridge—is perpetually waving.

In youth we wave back to the figure on the cliff.

I remember us on the bench together drinking warm Coke from the same bottle, two beings about to plunge into their own lives. How soon would we reach the bottom? While at the university in California my class read *The Odyssey*. It interested me because it's not only about the sea but about love and recognition. My father is like Odysseus, but so is my mother. Odysseus is Everyman. All seas lead to one home or another. Every path is the right one. And Magda has disappeared from the earth.

Now, in America, where I have made a home for myself, it is fall, the season of memory. The old car leans to one side. It, too, has strayed from time; it has no designations. It is a car only in name, but in essence it is a sigh.

The sky is beginning to darken. I can imagine my wife napping back at our house. Light spills from a kitchen window on to a patch of flowers.

When my father and I first met Magda at the airport years ago, she was clutching a naked doll with no hair. My father was not expecting a stick-thin girl with one arm, and so he scooped her up and whispered something in her ear. As we twisted our way home along cliffs, Magda looked out at England and then at me, as though I was somehow responsible—as though I had woven everything for her.

Only since becoming an adult have I realized how scared she must have been. She was a child in a place where she could not communicate. Over time her fear became trust and we became a family. When a person is loved, they are granted the strength of all seas.

She never spoke of the violence and abandonment of her early life. It's amazing she even went back. She bore deep scars but through loving turned them into rivers. For some people, life is the process of knocking through walls to get out. For others, it is the building of walls. My father once found Magda crying next to a one-thousand-year-old oak tree not far from the house. She had packed a child's suitcase, though its contents were splayed around her feet. He carried her into the house, and she continued weeping in our room.

That night she admitted her compulsion to escape. She was worried that if my father drowned, or I disappeared, she would be left with nothing. By running away at least she would have the joy of knowing she was missed.

A few days later my father took her on a "father-daughter trip" to London, explaining that he was going to introduce her to our relatives so she might never feel alone. The night they returned after the five-hour drive, we lay in bed together—her hairless doll between us. She explained in broken English how my father had taken her to the monkey cage at London Zoo and introduced her as "Magda the Invincible."

She once told me how she could feel the missing part of her arm—how she sometimes experienced the sensation of a hand—that it is possible to feel something without its physical presence.

Perhaps love is like this and we are all limbs of one giant intangible body. I can see her chopped black hair upon the pillow and remember kissing her shoulder as she slept.

Night can unmoor so many feelings; it is a relief we sleep through it. Night unravels the day and reinvents it for the first time.

We may mean nothing to time, but to each other we are kings and queens, and the world is a wild benevolent garden filled with chance meetings and unexplained departures.

Magda became so worried that my father would drown in a storm that one morning he woke us up as the world was beginning to crack open. With a special kind of paint Magda and I wrote our names on his surfboard. As we drifted back to sleep—the sound of the Land Rover roaring to life outside in the rain—an umbilical cord of light beneath our bedroom door held the world together.

After leaving for Poland, Magda wrote to my father once a week for two years and stopped when my mother returned from Australia—her skin several shades darker, a cigarette quivering between her lips as she stood before my father in the doorway. I was living in America when my mother appeared and know that my father took her in with no explanation. My mother had been away for eighteen years. She was actually surprised that I was gone, that I had grown up.

She never knew Magda, though I imagine she harbored the same kind of jealousy toward her as my wife does—a strange contempt because it is welcomed by me and probably by my father.

In the gloaming as I open the door of the abandoned car, Magda sings to me through the grinding of iron hinges. I sit inside. The steering wheel is a circle of bone and the chassis rocks with gratitude as I make an indentation in the seat. I am here and inhabit this moment, but I am forever on that wooden seat with Magda, or watching her release steaming eggs from their hot shells.

* * *

I never saw her after she left for Poland, but in the letters she wrote in the early years, it sounded as though she was happy. Once she even drew a stork on the envelope.

I know she missed us and that somehow we had given her the ability to live—that my father and I had untied a knot.

And now she is gone. I am not curious as to how it happened; that will come with the telephone call from my breathless father in the early hours of the morning.

I wonder if Magda passed my dreaming wife on her way.

I have encountered thousands of people only once, but they carry a memory of me and everyone else—like sand on a beach, shaping the edge of a living world.

When I arrive home from my walk, it is late and I am drowning in moonlight. I can smell hot coins of rain collecting in the sky, ready to fall. I can see my wife sitting on the porch swing smoking a joint. The smoke twists upward from her mouth, and, dissipating, it slides over the roof, above the empty forgotten car and the wildflowers, climbing, circling, giving itself to the unknown.

I approach. It begins to rain. My wife looks at me in the same way my mother must have looked at my father. She pats the cushion next to her. The seat takes on the weight of my body, and we both begin to laugh uncontrollably—as if simultaneously realizing that everything is a beautiful trick.

The final moments of her life. Marie-Françoise lay crushed under tons of rubble.

The fish she had been eating was still in her mouth.

Her eyes would not open.

She could sense the darkness that encapsulated her. She could not feel her body, as though during the fall, her soul had slipped out and lay waiting for the exact moment when it would disappear from the world.

Then her life, like a cloud, split open, and she lay motionless in a rain of moments.

The green telephone in her grandparents' kitchen next to the plant.

She could feel the cool plastic of the handle and the sensation of cupping it under her ear. She could hear a voice at the other end of the line that she recognized as her own.

The weight of her mother's shoes as she carried them into the bedroom.

The idea that one day she'd be grown-up and would have to wear such things.

Running into a friend.

That time had passed.

And then the rain of her life stopped, and she was in darkness, her heart pushing slowly against her ribs. Muted noise as though she were underwater.

Then the rain of moments began again until she was drenched by single esoteric details:

Morning light behind the curtain.

The smell of classrooms.

A glass of milk.

The hope for a father and the imagined pressure of his arms against her.

Laying her head upon her new boyfriend's cool back in the morning. She had done it twice. It was as important as being born.

Her grandparents again, but characters in their own stories—walking barefoot in the snowy mud and stepping on a buried hand.

The end of the war.

A bungalow in France.

A daughter.

A granddaughter.

Her mother's elbows as she drove their old brown Renault.

Marie-Françoise could not feel her body and was unable to shout.

There was no sound, nothing stirred but the silent movies projected on the inside of her skull.

She was not so much aware that she was dying as she was that she was still alive. Had she more time, she may have nurtured a hope of being rescued. Instead, memory leaked out around her.

Blowing out candles unsuccessfully—birthday year insignificant, just the aroma of smoke as small fires were extinguished by tiny helping breaths.

Then the sound of footsteps in the hall, and creeping barefoot to find her grandfather dead at the kitchen table with the refrigerator door open.

An egg unbroken on the floor.

Her grandmother's screams.

This memory was not painful to her now. Her life was an open window and she a butterfly.

If not for her intermittent returns to darkness—the body's insistence on life—she could have been on vacation, swimming underwater, each stroke of her arms in the cool water a complete philosophy.

And then she smelled her grandmother's coat, hanging loyally behind the kitchen door with a bag of bags and a broom.

She wondered if she had lived her entire life from under the collapsed building. That her life was imagined by a self she'd never fully known.

And then with the expediency of the dying, she immediately fell in love with the darkness and the eight seconds she had left in it—each second like a mouthful of food to a starving man.

APPLES

As night unraveled through the streets of Brooklyn, the sign outside Serge's shoe repair shop glowed. The red neon burned through evening and into early morning. Anyone pacing the city, anyone lingering in the palm of a streetlight could not ignore the dazzle and low growl of bright gas pumped through tubes like blood in the shape of letters—a promise to all who passed that certain things never need go unmended.

Below the neon sign, Serge's display consisted of several pairs of shoes whose owners had never returned. Serge had painstakingly reconstructed them into sullen models of their former selves.

Under a shelf of dusty Russian magazines was a broken chair for customers to wait while Serge hammered, glued, and stitched. The smell of glue was often overpowering, but it was a thick, fragrant odor that hypnotized customers into waiting quietly in their socks.

The broken chair would not have supported the full weight of a person, but by some miracle had remained intact, beautifully ancient, with one leg suspended an inch above the carpet, as though immersed in a never-ending dream of walking.

Serge was a large Russian with a face like old leather and eyes that over time had been dulled by life. When he was a young man, his hairy arms and beastlike stature were enough to pique the interests of men who enjoyed fistfights. But Serge always backed away from the sly remarks of drunkards, so they assumed him dull-witted or a coward, of which he was neither.

Serge was learning English slowly like an old man entering a sea. He enjoyed it because there were so many secrets entrenched within the meanings and in the pronunciation of each strange word.

Like butterflies, new words flew from Serge's mouth and fluttered about the classroom for everyone to admire.

Serge had taken an English class at a local Russian Orthodox Church, designed after its famous cousin in Saint Petersburg. Serge often overheard neighborhood children discussing the rumor that the church had partly been constructed out of chocolate.

One evening in class, after the teacher had asked everybody's profession, she winked at Serge and explained to the class how the word for the bottom of a shoe and the name for a person's spirit were pronounced without any difference.

That night Serge lay awake beneath a full moon in his bed. His curtains were ivory squares that washed his crumbling apartment white, turning furniture to old wedding cake.

He repeated the word he'd learned in class. He said it out loud from the soft canyon of his pillow. Night had passed, but it was not yet morning.

Serge stopped going to class three weeks later because he couldn't keep his eyes open. He arrived early for his final class and explained to the teacher that it may have been the glue he used in his shop, but he just couldn't stop falling asleep. She was sad to see him leave and advised him to read newspapers in English. Other students drifted in, and within twenty minutes, Serge fell into a deep pool of sleep and then quickly resurfaced in a dream. He was back in Russia. There was a light wind. He entered his family house, and several birds escaped through the open door slapping his head with their wings.

As his classmates practiced the sounds and shapes of their desires, Serge climbed the dark stairs of the house his grandfather had repaired as a teenager. The house had once been the center of village life, where Serge's grandfather held great parties with tall cakes, apple beer, and incense that hung from the fireplace in tight, dry bundles.

A river curled across the property, and Serge's grandfather died one day beside it, while drawing a bird, which he abandoned to a life without flight. Serge had been watching him from the parlor window and, like several village children running through the orchard, had thought the old man to be dozing.

For two blissful years, Serge lived in the old house with his wife, a dark-haired seamstress from a village across the mountain where water froze all year-round.

She died in childbirth almost one year after Serge's grandfather. The birth of his daughter was the saddest-happiest day of his life.

The grand old house soon declined, and within a short time only several of its rooms were comfortably habitable. Their only visitors were a motley group of animals that crept up to the back door at dusk. Serge deposited scraps in several piles to prevent disputes. Serge held his daughter up to the kitchen window so she could see.

While Serge's mostly Russian classmates chained letters to one another, he continued to dream and breathlessly reached the top floor of a house now boarded up and empty. From down the hall, he could hear his daughter crying, but when he tried to move in her direction, an invisible force held him in place. Like all parents, Serge recognized the nuances of his daughter's anguish, and of all the things she could have been crying for; the dream—in a stroke of illusory genius—had merely soiled her diaper.

Serge had often spent whole nights perched over her crib like a gargoyle, afraid for the worst. In Greek myth, Death and Sleep are brothers.

Had it not been for his daughter's crying, Serge would have been afraid and the dream would have been a nightmare—an expression Serge loved because night was like a horse that tore through the forest of memory.

As Serge cupped the doorknob and entered, the crying from down the hall abruptly ceased. In darkness on the broken chair from Serge's shoe repair shop was his grandfather.

As he approached the suited figure, the old man's left foot ascended through a constellation of dust. His eyes glowed like two small moons; his sole had come unstitched.

Under the spell of the dream, Serge knelt down to inspect the damage. His tools appeared.

Only once in his life had Serge repaired a sole that bore the weight of a foot. His grandfather once confessed that such an operation required such skilled stitching and steadiness of hand that it should only be attempted as an act of trust—and reminded Serge of the peasants who tended the feet of Jesus.

Serge's grandfather had not only repaired shoes but also crafted them from pungent sheets of leather and small hunks of oak.

One snowy morning in 1903, a guard from the palace of Prince Romanov rode into the village, his legs numb with frostbite. Across his shoulder in a black satchel threaded with gold were thousands of rubles and a cast of the six-year-old prince's feet.

The guard dismounted wearily and then announced to the growing crowd how the great gilded hall of the royal palace had resounded with the name of *their* local shoemaker. Serge's grandfather was summoned immediately from his smoky cottage on the edge of town. On his arrival, the guard fell to his knees and begged him to make the shoes his masters had sent him to procure. Serge's grandfather helped him up from the muddy puddle and then listened as the guard explained how, with so much money in his satchel, it was unlikely he'd make it back to the palace alive, and in the event of his disappearance, his wife and child would have to live with eternal shame.

Serge's grandfather was kind, and he assured the guard that he would make the shoes and that for the time it took to craft each piece he would share their home. The palace guard lived in the shoemaker's cottage for two months and, over steaming potatoes, told stories of bravery and last words from the frozen battlefields of Russia's battlefronts.

As Serge stitched his grandfather's phantom shoe, the old man vanished, leaving behind only a few crumbs of soil on the floorboards. The dream, however, remained intact, and he could hear the old man descending the staircase—the chair dragging behind him and clapping each step.

When Serge awoke, class was almost at an end, and the dream slipped from his memory like a pebble sucked back into the sea.

Several months after the dream in that last English class, Serge sat quietly on a B63 bus, watching various workmen settle into their labor for the day. The bus swerved to avoid craterlike potholes. Serge balanced an elaborate lunch on his lap. He had ordered it the night before from a Polish restaurant on the corner of his block. It was a special day, and on the seat next to him was his finest suit wrapped in paper and tied with string.

Although the day's heat was still settling, dark bruises drifted across the sky, stopping above the river to admire themselves. It was a day Serge had been looking forward to all winter, and after opening the shop he unlocked the nightly drop box and set to work on the first pair of shoes—looking up only to greet customers with unusual verve.

It was the day of Brooklyn's only apple festival, and for blocks, in apartments of all shapes and sizes, children were cleaning out buckets and stuffing their pockets with bags in preparation for the evening affair. The ragged homeless had gathered on the corner and were idly watching the stream of commuters disappear into the subway, occasionally asking one of them for a cigarette.

By early afternoon, rain lashed the front window. It was thick and sticky in the shop, especially when the machines were running at full tilt. Moisture in the air prevented the glue from sticking with its usual tenacity. Serge wiped the sweat from his forehead with a corner of his apron. He counted how many pairs of shoes were left to fix and then conducted a triage, placing the most critical repairs at the front of the line.

Each finished pair was wrapped in a white muslin cloth and hung from one of thirty nails hammered unevenly into the back wall with a Russian bootheel.

A small boy from one of the nearby slums often visited Serge at the shop. Omar lived in a damp apartment with his aunt, who had several children of her own. Omar didn't know where his parents were, and his aunt refused to tell him until he was eighteen years old. Omar had once pointed out that Serge's back wall of shoes could easily have been a hiding place for a "spider's future meals."

Serge asked Omar to point to out which package looked most suspicious. Omar chose a lumpy white bundle hanging from the farthest, highest nail. Grumbling, Serge took his footstool and plucked it from the nail. He set it in front of Omar and unraveled the cloth. Omar turned up his nose and remarked that it was the biggest fly or the ugliest pair of shoes he had ever seen.

Serge could not remember a time Omar had visited and not pleaded with him to teach him the business of shoes or at the very least let him try his hand on the polishing machine.

"Shoes," Omar once proclaimed, "are the heart's messengers."

Serge chuckled and told him to scram but later wrote the phrase down on some muslin cloth and taped it to the old bathroom mirror.

Omar had not been to the shop since July fourteenth—almost a month. Serge knew this because he marked Omar's visits on the calendar by drawing a pair of round faces: a small head with a smile and a big head with a straight line for a mouth.

Serge's only other friend was a blind tobacconist from Ukraine called Peter, who when not being beaten by his wife played obsolete military songs on an accordion.

Serge sewed the final stitches on a roller skate, as though he were playing a tiny violin. After breaking and tying the thread, Serge held the skate up to the light and inspected each stitch. One of the wheels began to spin. Serge imagined himself on the wheel, spinning through life, moving through time but never actually getting anywhere.

It only seemed like yesterday that small broken wings of snow had silently fallen against the shop window; only yesterday he'd boiled his daughter's diapers on a frozen winter morning in Russia. Without memory, time would be no use to mankind, Serge thought.

Many years ago, his grandfather had bought him a pair of ice skates to use on the river when it froze. In the arms of an afternoon snowfall, his grandfather told him that happiness tears the sky to pieces.

Serge could almost feel his grandfather's hot, smoky breath against his cheek; then a view of the apple orchard; each tree propped on the white tablecloth and the indentations of animals' feet; the hollow bark of an owl through the white falling drops.

On a tattered poster behind the door of Serge's shop was a giant shoe elevated above the heads of several shoe mechanics. They were pointing to the sole and marveling. As a young man, Serge had dreamed of coming to America and purchasing a Cadillac or a Lincoln, like the ones important Mafiosi cherished. About the time he married, Serge daydreamed on dry summer afternoons in the orchard with his back

against a tree. The apple trees were always stuffed with birds, and
Serge often fell asleep to their evening concert, while his wife dug
flower beds barefoot.

He imagined himself cruising down Fifth Avenue, the sparkling
dashboard before him, his children reading American magazines in
the backseat. Their feet, of course, fitted with the finest Italian leather
shoes and their voices light and full of hope.

His wife died a few months later while giving birth to their daughter. Six months and one week after that, doctors from a nearby city explained to Serge that his daughter had a heart full of holes and that she
wouldn't last the summer. The doctors agreed that the only two things
capable of saving her life were God and money. Serge immediately put
the house up for sale, but by the time it sold, it was too late.

Serge removed a small tongue of gum from the roller skate's wheel
with a razor. He bit his lip so hard that blood ran down his chin and
dripped into a pile of laces. Thirty years later, the shame of how he'd
wished away all his money on a car still burned his cheeks.

On a windless day in July, Serge's daughter was lowered into a small
hole at the edge of the family apple orchard. A white cross marked the
position of her head, upon which gold script told anyone who cared to
pass that she was her father's only daughter and that she loved animals. In the box at her feet, Serge placed the family tools, to give his
grandfather something to do while they waited for him.

He hung the roller skates from the longest, most crooked nail.

Outside, birds were pulling nets of song through the streets.

Morning's dark clouds had dispersed, leaving a blue shell of sky
lightly chalked.

With the skates mounted and the street outside noticeably busier, Serge decided to close up and make his way over to the apple harvest.

He dressed meticulously and combed his white hair in the yellowing toilet mirror. After polishing his own shoes on the machine in his socks, he washed his hands.

Under the sink was a long silver cake knife wrapped closely in white muslin cloth. It was a family heirloom and once guided the weight of two hands across a wedding cake.

Serge slipped the wedding knife into his pocket and flicked off all the lights inside. The outside sign burned all night in dazzling red neon read. It read: ALL SOLES FIXED HERE.

He locked up and stepped onto the street.

Serge hoped he might see Peter the blind tobacconist or Omar— someone to keep him from the company of ghosts. Children rushed past with buckets tied to their backs with rope. Others kept pace with their parents, their faces sour with the embarrassment of a public scolding.

Like a gust of wind, another group of children swept past Serge, gently brushing the edges of his clothing.

The evening was comfortably warm, and for miles around, the piercing freshness of ripe apples poured into people's homes like sunlight.

Serge lived humbly in a basement apartment in the Greenpoint section of Brooklyn. His landlord, who lived upstairs, was a retired university professor who thumped on the floor with a broom when he listened to Beethoven. He was also a widower and the only member of his family to escape the Nazi gas chambers. The weight of their sadness combined would have been too much for either to bear, and so their relationship consisted of a mutual nod whenever they came face-to-face.

On a table next to Serge's bed was a small apple tree, which he tended to every day as responsively as if it had been a dying companion. He purchased the most expensive plant foods to ensure its prosperity. It was almost a foot tall and, with a growing confidence in the world around it, had begun to widen at its base.

In three months, depending on the weather, Serge would have to sneak down to a once-abandoned lot, rip up some cracked tarmac with a crowbar, and plant the tree next to all the others he had planted since arriving in Brooklyn in 1974. After thirty years the wasteland lot had become an orchard and the site of New York City's only apple festival.

Nearing the orchard, Serge could hear the crowd and wondered if there would be anywhere to set up his folding chair.

As he turned the final corner, his perpetually dry eyes were suddenly moist and he felt himself crying. Instead of stopping to forage for a handkerchief, Serge continued his slow rocking walk, for he was sure that no one would look at him long enough to know.

On the eve of his departure from the small Russian village of his birth, Serge had smoked in the family orchard watching workmen board up the windows of his family home with thick planks. The men's wives toiled inside, covering furniture with thick white sheets as though blindfolding them.

Before the men nailed shut the front door, Serge carried his suitcase outside and set it on the grass. It was dusk. The river that flowed across the property was high and thick with the soft black bones of trees.

Like people, all rivers are falling.

With several blankets borrowed from his mother-in-law, Serge made a bed for himself on the grass, six feet above his child.

At dawn, with a film of dew upon his skin and clothes, Serge rose to his knees in order to kiss the gravestone one final time. However, at some moment during the night, an apple had swollen just enough to sit perfectly on the head of the stone. Serge was breathless and picked the apple so the branch—madly and gratefully—could return to the tangle of branches above. He buried the apple deep in his suitcase. On the journey west, six days of hunger and thirst were not enough to tempt him to eat it.

As Serge came within sight of the lot, he was confronted once again with his daughter's legacy and more than a hundred Russian apple trees nodded in recognition.

The curling limbs of the trees were studded with apples, and children grew within the branches, laughing and hanging upside down.

Serge unfolded his chair at the edge of the orchard and listened to the sound of apples punching buckets. Some people had brought barbeques and were baking apples wrapped in aluminium foil.

After several hours, Serge cut his last slice of apple with the silver wedding knife and then wrapped the knife back in muslin cloth. People were beginning to go home. Children dispersed in small groups, their tiny backs bent over with cargoes of fruit. An apple is the size and weight of a human heart; they were carrying the hearts of those not yet born and those lost forever.

It was getting chilly and Serge didn't want to risk his arthritic hands. By morning, his nightly drop box was sure to be full of broken soles and heels worn into smiles.

As he started to rise, Omar pushed through the crowd, his pockets so stuffed with apples that he could only run with his legs straight.

"Shoe-man!" he exclaimed. "I've been looking for you all night."

At the end of the block a firecracker exploded, and Omar grinned.

"Up to your old mischief, uh?" Serge said.

"I bought you a baked apple, but I dropped it and a dog ate it." Omar arranged the apples stuffed into his pants.

"The mayor of New York was here, did you see him?" Omar asked. Serge said no.

"Someone threw an apple at him," Omar said, laughing.

"Not you, I hope," Serge muttered.

"No, not me—but he said that the city has bought the lot and is giving the orchard to the children of New York." Omar lunged for an apple as it popped free from his pocket and rolled under Serge's chair.

"Who do you think planted these trees, Omar?" Serge asked. "Haven't you ever wondered who started this?"

Omar was on the ground fishing for the lost apple but managed to say, "Nobody knows who did it. The mayor said it's one of the city's great mysteries."

"But have you ever wondered why anyone would do such a thing?" Serge asked.

"Because they love apples," Omar said.

Serge noticed the moon and felt the deep pull of home.

When Omar finally found the apple under the chair, he removed one of his little socks and ripped it in half.

"What are you doing down there?" Serge snapped.

A pair of small hands suddenly began to skate over Serge's shoes. The hands moved vigorously but with controlled strength. Omar spat on the sock and rubbed the heel. Serge tried to get up and shake off the scoundrel, but he had already started the other shoe. Serge sat back and closed his eyes.

EVERYDAY THINGS

For a moment after waking up, Thomas was only vaguely aware that
he was alive. Then, like the shock of cold water hitting his body,
Thomas remembered that his wife's sister had telephoned during the
night, that they had spoken briefly and nothing had been resolved.

He lifted the blanket off his body and waded through a gray light
that had seeped through the curtains and into the room. He looked at
the telephone with disbelief and then made a pot of tea. While it was
brewing, he sat on his bed and fought to remember a dream. He tried
piecing it together, but it was as though a feast had taken place during the night in his honor and he had awoken with only a few crumbs.
He looked at the telephone again.

He could hear rain spraying the window and decided to write his
letter of resignation. He sat at his desk. He swept aside bills and the
report he would never finish, then pulled a crisp sheet of paper from
the bed of the printer. After finishing a cup of tea, he began to write.
He could feel a skin of sugar upon his teeth and after writing his own

address, realized he could not steady his hand. It shook like a small, dying animal.

He turned his head toward the telephone but did not look.

Outside, he could hear the increasing traffic. People were going to work, radios were clicking to life in bedrooms, coffee was dripping into glass jugs, bathtubs were filling up. He gripped the handle of the teapot awkwardly and poured himself another cup.

He could imagine his wife in the hospital, her limp body beneath the white sheet like a spread of mountains. In his mind's eye, he pictured the nurse's white shoes and his wife's bare feet parted beneath the hospital sheets.

Her sister had called in the early hours, but he had spoken very little because each time he thought of a word, it had popped like a bubble before he could nudge it past his teeth and into the telephone. Nothing had been resolved, and he thought of the hospital corridor, a long river of plastic with brightly colored lines upon the floor. He could sense the tension in her sister's voice as she imparted everything the doctors had told her. All he could think was how beautiful the word *triage* was.

He dressed. The house was cold and quiet. He poured himself more tea and drank it cold. As he poked his arms through the sleeves of his jacket, his eye caught a pair of her boots. He wanted to slip his hands inside, through the dark leather mouths and into the stomachs that cradled her feet.

He tried calling her sister. Her telephone rang for a long time. He replaced the receiver, feeling that life was disordered in a way he had never imagined.

He looked at his watch and thought of his old self driving to work, listening to the news, sipping coffee. He felt a strange sense of shame and naivety and knew that if he let his mind regress, it would pass a countless number of occasions in which he could have been a stronger and brighter version of himself.

After tying his shoes, he reached into the closet for his raincoat. Instead of yanking it from the hanger, he tugged slightly at the arm and felt his hand begin to wander. It brushed against different fabrics and then stopped at her favorite coat, a long camel-hair one with a thick belt. His fingers crawled into the pocket and swam around between coins, slips of paper, and mints. The secrets of a hand.

He drove to the hospital. The hand that had been in her coat pocket exuded a light aroma of perfume. He thought of her spa and pictured the shelf of tiny bottles above her desk, each one containing a distilled floral essence, each bottle an olfactory fingerprint.

He remembered the faces of her clients as they hung their coats and then peeled a magazine from the stack on the table. He remembered watching their eyes sail slowly through the pages as they anticipated the warm, scented oil upon their faces and the soothing calligraphy of his wife's hands.

The road to the hospital became narrow and straight. It stretched through a forest like a gray bookmark, and dead leaves—like brittle letters—bounced across the highway on their brittle ends.

He tried to hold a portrait of her face in his mind but could not weave each detail simultaneously. He thought again of the small bottles above her desk.

At the hospital he stood above her and listened. Birds muttered on the window ledge, a machine clicked. He sat in a chair and studied her fingers. They were long and evenly spaced. On her wrist was a clear plastic band with her name written by a computer. This made him angry. He leaned in and breathed upon her hand. It was warm, and he shuddered as his breath pushed against her skin.

He felt numb, as though during the night his body had been filled with plaster. He wondered what was happening inside her head. He imagined a garden with the noisy dots of birds.

The day of the operation had been the worst day. Now it was a waiting game, said her sister.

After napping, he awoke to a shadow cast over his wife's body.

"Good morning, Thomas," the nurse said.

He nodded and asked if there was any change in her condition. The nurse consulted her charts and replied that there was no change.

"Would you like to wash her face?" the nurse asked. He turned to his sleeping wife and imagined swishing a wet cloth through the tiny canyons and then across the plains of her cheeks. He felt awkward and his hands turned to wood.

"I'll get you some warm water," the nurse said.

She returned a moment later and placed a bowl and some cotton balls beside his wife's bed. Thomas dipped a ball of cotton into the warm water and then squeezed it. He swished it along her forehead. She did not move. When he had finished, he patted her face with a soft towel, being careful not to cover her mouth or nose.

The operation had lasted six hours and twelve minutes. During this time, Thomas left the hospital and walked to a park where he sat on a bench and wept violently for several minutes. He then smoked a cigarette and watched two boys throw a football to one another. In the December twilight, a dog barked. Then the park was swallowed by darkness. As he had walked back to the hospital, he felt ashamed that he had left even for a moment and wondered if her sister would be angry with him.

He stood before the automatic doors at the hospital for a moment before continuing.

As he had made his way back to her room, he remembered the boys playing football in the park. He thought to himself that one year from this moment, everything would be different—for better or worse.

The nurse returned and took away the bowl and cotton balls. Thomas remembered his wife's voice from years ago, expressing a wish to see the lavender fields of France.

Next year for definite, he thought, when all this is behind us, we'll do something like that.

Four days since the operation, and everyone who visited commented on how she had lost weight, as though it were somehow complimentary. It was an uncommonly warm afternoon, and Thomas decided to walk to the park again. It felt good to walk, and he tried to imagine the splintering glass, the spontaneous explosion of the air bag—her face and crumpling body.

He saw the park up ahead and slackened his pace. He tried to see the faces of people driving past him. They eyed him for a split second and were gone.

A sudden loathing filled him.

As he sat down on an empty bench he resisted an urge to sprint back to the hospital and carry her from the bed to their house and then lock all the doors.

At that moment, Thomas realized he had changed, that he was not the same man, but like everyone else, he was the result of an accident that had once taken place between nature and chance.

An old woman with hanging cheeks sat down beside him and sighed.

"The evenings have become so cold," she said. She offered him a stick of violet gum. He slipped it into his mouth and chewed. They sat mostly in silence.

"This time next year," Thomas suddenly remarked to the woman, "my wife and I will be in France."

"Oh, that's nice, dear." The old lady seemed delighted but then looked away. "My husband and I always talked about going to Europe."

"They grow lavender and you can smell it in the air as you amble through the villages," Thomas said.

"Wished we'd gone when we had the chance," she said, "but life just swallows you up, doesn't it? Just swallows you up with its everyday things."

That evening at the hospital, Thomas insisted that he stay with his wife—that he hold her hand and burn some of her favorite distilled essences.

"Most people go home, get a good night's sleep, and come back first thing," the nurse said as she folded a towel.

"I'm not most people," Thomas said and truly meant it. The nurse left the room without a word.

CONCEPTION

I am sitting at the kitchen table with the lights off. There is broken glass strewn across the red stone floor. The back door is wide open, and moonlight drips through the trees and pools in the doorway. I am sitting at the table drinking tea in darkness, while my wife is somewhere in the fields that stretch endlessly behind our house. I hold the cup with both hands, as though engaged in holiness. I can imagine her in mud up to her ankles, her glasses spotted with rain, hair breaking like black sea on her shoulders.

When I arrived home and saw the broken glass and the open door, I knew she had received news from the doctors. Flapping in the breeze on the table like a white tongue is the letter, which may confirm her worst fear. I dare not read it. In the darkness I can see the cluster of words scattered across the page; like small fallen bodies they reach out for us.

I wonder if she smashed the glass on purpose or if one of her walking poles nudged it as she twisted her back and thrashed all limbs, negotiating her crutches like giant chopsticks as she made for the empty, moonlit pasture.

Her legs are so deformed you'd think they were rubber. I touched them for the first time on our wedding night at a bed-and-breakfast only eight miles up the mountain. On a clear day you can see it from behind our cottage. I remember the bed and the crisp, yellowing sheets. I wondered how many people had slept in it. I marveled at how the pillow, like a small theater, had staged countless dreams. At dusk, when I smoke in the garden, the lights of the bed-and-breakfast flutter beneath a faint flock of stars and remind me of our first night. We touched with a softness that pushed through the skin into memory, like arms plunged into a river—we could feel the weight of each other's stones.

My wife's legs are so unnaturally twisted that when she was a girl her classmates boasted of frequent nightmares in which their own legs melted into dead white snakes. And they called her names that pierced her like arrows. Every night she fell asleep bleeding and dreaming that one morning she would awake with legs as straight and strong as trees and that on Saturday morning small pink fingers would push the doorbell—a prelude to the breathless voices calling her out to play.

My father was a miner. Her father was a welder who repaired steel-frame supports in the shafts. She dreamed that when her bones woke up and joined hands, her father would light his welding torch and turn her poles into a bicycle with a basket on the front, the sort other girls used to ferry hot parcels of fish-and-chips or crab apples poached from a tree by throwing sticks into the branches.

Once, she threw her poles into the branches of a pear tree that grew at the edge of the schoolyard. They stuck, and when the bell rang summoning children back to their cold desks, she sat shivering outside until a teacher noticed a speck by the fence and sent for the caretaker and his retarded son, who dragged the ladder across the yard pulling faces to the window of every classroom.

My wife is out in the fields, in the shadow of a mountain crowned by mist. Perhaps she is leaning against a stile and watches the drifting cows, their eyes as still and black as well water.

The village we live in erupted from mud, and mothers wage an impossible war against the perpetually dissolving ground. Above the village, the sky is so stuffed with cloud that water, like some curious animal, finds its way into everything and lives on the backs of the people —slowly drowning them.

On Saturday the unmarried and the widowed kiss and fight at the Castle Pub on the hill. Anyone not at the pub or in the ground is sprawled before blazing fires in cottages, which, like sad ornaments, dangle upon the hillsides on smoky threads. Children watch black-and-white televisions in kitchens as fathers chop heads off fish and smoke cigarettes, peering into back gardens until evening, like a grieving stranger pulls his cloak across the day.

My tea is cold, and the moon, anchored by the hopes and wishes of those abandoned souls churning their way home from the pub, has drifted deeper into the sky.

My wife and I have been back and forth to Wrexham Hospital in the rusting truck. They slide a needle into her spine, which like lightning splits me in two.

And there's the letter that I daren't read, because I have wanted a son since my father was crushed in a collapsed shaft.

I was a boy in this very kitchen, perched at the table in darkness waiting for him to come home and take me to the fair. I had my heart set on the acquisition of small orange fish, which were being dispensed liberally to children in thin plastic bags.

When suppertime passed and my father was still not home, I was so angry that I drew a picture of him and then stabbed it with my pencil. I pictured him at the pub, his face smeared with coal dust, sitting quietly with his workmates rolling cigarettes.

Eventually, a neighbor knocked and entered. She set a plastic Thermos of soup in front of me and explained how my father was stuck in a mine and that it would be on the news. I thought of the drawing and cried.

My mother waited at the entrance to the shaft for three days, and I slept at the neighbor's house beneath a crucifix made from clothes pegs. I imagined myself wandering the grassy mountainside and then digging with the pencil I'd used to stab my father until his hand pushed through the soil holding a bag of fish.

My wife is the neighbor's daughter. Before the night my father died, I'd only seen her on Sunday afternoons tilting around her front garden like a broken toy.

She told me that while my father's body might be crushed under tons of black earth, the body is nothing but camouflage. She whispered that every soul is a river trying to find its way back to the sea.

I have wanted a son since my father's accident. I will continue where he left off. I hoped I was the crucial link. When I can bury every ounce of my disappointment about what I think the letter says, I will slip through the gate into the fields and bring her home. I never want

her to know that fatherhood was the ambition of my life. I don't want
her to feel as though she has let me down; yet for a moment I consider
what would happen if I packed a small bag and escaped, perhaps to
London where I could work on a market, or up to Scotland where I'd
mine deep lochs for eels. It's tempting to imagine how we could hurt
someone close, because it reminds us how fiercely we love them.

In this very kitchen I would listen to my mother tell stories about
my dead father. The Sunday afternoon they drove up Sugar Loaf and
listened to the crackling radio with a blanket spread over their legs. It
had rained, she said, and I imagined the beads of water on the windshield like a thousand eyes, or each drop a small imperfect reflection
of a perfect moment. She told me about their first weekend away in
Blackpool, fishing for crabs off the pier with cans of beer and hot
sausages wrapped in newspaper. She told me that love is when a person introduces you to yourself for the first time.

After he died, I began to imagine the deformed girl from next door
as my lover. I imagined driving her up Sugar Loaf Mountain on the
back of my bicycle and then touching her legs, and then kissing them
with the coyness of snowfall. I imagined defending her in the play-
ground, and with my pillow I practiced punching the rubbery noses of
my schoolmates should they dare open their mouths and spill ugliness
upon her.

Years ago, I wrote to doctors in America and asked how much it
would cost to straighten her legs. Every single one of them wrote back
requesting charts, personal information, and, most importantly, photographs. The only photographs I had of her legs I took surreptitiously
while she was asleep. I sent them all. There is nothing they can do now,

they said, but advances in technology are made every day, and I should keep in touch—which I secretly do. Every Christmas twelve doctors across America each receive a package of tea from Wales.

But if she were whole and her legs were capable of symmetry, I would no longer lift her in and out of the bath, nor drive her to the library where she stamps books and enrolls new members, for these are rituals of marriage in which I lose myself.

I imagine if she were like everyone else: scrambling from the truck on Sugar Loaf Mountain to chase one another. It would take ten years off our lives to run like that. All couples should run away from each other and then collapse in a knot.

Everyone in the village knows me as they knew my father. Once my wife took some coal from the burner and smeared a little dust on my face. She told me I look like him—that our eyes contain the same color water. Death ends a life but not a relationship.

I sweep up the glass on the red stone floor, then find my rubber boots. She won't have eaten. I will carry her home and then lower her into a hot bath. She will cry, and I will say nothing.

It is almost midnight and wind throws light rain against the cottage, whipping the windows and softening cemented stones. The ground beneath the gate has been churned by the split hooves of cows. The mud is thick with puddles as deep as buckets.

As the ground begins to harden I hear the frantic call of some animal. The pasture is free of cows and glistens like wedding cake. As I trudge across it, I notice a white speck in the middle and realize that the noise is the sound of my wife's laughter.

I quicken my step and begin to pant. Drops of rain, silvered momentarily by moonlight, plummet through white plumes of my breath like stars.

My wife is standing without her poles and for an instant I suspect a miracle, but as I approach I see that she is up to her knees in mud and that her poles have been tossed out of reach by the same passion that makes her laugh.

Before I embrace her, I turn around. Mist has swallowed the house. Only the white field and our two shaking bodies inhabit the earth.

As I fall to my knees and reach for her torso, I feel her fingers press against my scalp. Her voice is light and powerful.

"The letter," she says. I try to pull her from the mud, but it holds her as though it were holding its first flower.

"Did you read the letter?" she says again.

"I don't care about that anymore," I say, but a burst of wind carries away the words and she laughs again, lifting her arms to the sky as though channeling some great force through her body.

SAVE AS MANY

AS YOU RUIN

By the time Gerard leaves the office it has stopped snowing. Lights are coming on, but it's not yet dark. At the end of each block the sidewalk disappears under a pool of gray ice water.

Gerard thinks of everyone's footprints in the snow. Manhattan was once a forest. He imagines the footprints of an Indian slipping home, on his shoulders a warm carcass with clumps of snow stuck to its fur.

Gerard thinks of his own footprints and how soon they will disappear. He exhales into the world and his breath disappears. He recalls Rilke, *what is ours floats into the air, like steam from a dish of hot food.* He wonders if his life is an extraordinary one.

Gerard remembers the freezing cross-country races at his English prep school. Bare white legs spotted with mud. Plum-sized hearts thumping.

He remembers Hetherington, the physical education teacher, his strong jaw and sweet blue eyes—the desire to see his boys drink up the glory of victory. Hetherington ran in the 1936 Olympics in Berlin.

He won a medal. Hitler watched. Millions were about to be killed as a teenage Hetherington crossed the finish line. A few years later, children walked into gas ovens after a long journey from home. They were scared but trusted their parents.

Gerard feels stabbing love for his daughter. He crosses Fifty-third Street. Her name is Lucy, and she is eight. She has short brown hair with Hello Kitty clips pinned cleanly to her head. Gerard once sat next to a rabbi on the train to Southampton. The rabbi had just returned from England. He was making a documentary about the war.

"But there are so many already," Gerard had said.

Walking up Fifth Avenue he cringes at the insensitivity of his comment. He must have thought I was like everyone else, thinks Gerard. Am I like everyone else, he thinks. The rabbi had merely put his hand on Gerard's cuff for a moment.

It suddenly begins snowing again.

Yellow taxis are nodding through the snowy dusk. The lights from shopwindows are beckoning. Gerard thinks of the mannequins. They are very still, perfectly still. They are talking about something they've never done. They are sitting down to meals they'll never eat; tucked into beds in which they'll never dream.

He pictures Lucy in their warm apartment perched at the table reading a simplified *Black Beauty* in large print. Her legs are swinging under the table in concentration. He has never known such devotion.

Gerard is handsome. He has slept with many women. Most knew he would never love them, so they kept a distance, sparing themselves the grief of an ancient pain. Gerard loved one woman once, but not Lucy's mother.

Lucy is at home with Indira, a heavy-set Barnard student from New Delhi who cooks dinner every weeknight and helps Lucy with her homework. Gerard and Lucy love Indian food. Indira often stays and eats with them—at first she wouldn't. She is becoming part of the family. Her father died.

The snow is covering everything. Gerard remembers *The Invisible Man*. A crackling film from the 1930s. He watched it one night with Lucy. She'd seen it listed in *TV Guide* and wanted to watch it. It was on late. She fell asleep after five minutes. Gerard could feel her heart thudding like a soft, warm rock. As he carried her to bed, she asked him what happened to the invisible man. Gerard told her that he was caught because it began to snow and he left footprints. That's beautiful, she said, without opening her eyes.

It's a blizzard now.

Flakes like clumps of fur ripped from winter's back.

And then he sees Laurel through the falling snow.

Eight years have passed.

He can't believe it and stops walking.

A woman with bags bumps into him and curses.

Laurel is a few feet away.

He steps over to the glass and taps gently on it.

A line of people inside the shop turn to face him like a sleepy jury.

Her face is still sharp and angular like a Cubist painting, but softened now by her eyes, which have sunk or regressed partly into memory. He thinks she is more beautiful than ever. Her mouth opens in the shape of an almond. Gerard cannot tell if she is smiling.

All this happens within five seconds.

Gerard wonders if he has done the right thing. Perhaps he should have walked on. Later at home in his study, he could re-create the moment he saw her in line at the shop and let the memory spill over like a faucet left running.

She is holding a tray of raw fish and a bottle of iced tea. In that moment of recognition he is not consumed by a rushing sensation of love—quite simply a door opens to a room that has never gone away. The years apart were just years without one another.

They were together only a few months. They met at a dinner party given by one of Gerard's colleagues. There were candles, and wine, and the women wore dresses that left their shoulders bare. The candles made their shoulders glisten. Even unattractive women have beautiful shoulders. He and Laurel talked for hours. He felt as if they were catching up, though they'd never met.

When he finds her in the line she is about to pay, but Gerard quickly hands the cashier a few bills.

Laurel blushes.

"I can't believe it's you," she says.

"I know," he says and tries to maintain eye contact, but people are pushing past.

"So, how are you?" she says.

"Fine," he says. "And you?"

"Good," she says. "How is your daughter?"

"She's wonderful, just wonderful."

"How is her mother?"

Gerard pauses.

"Dead," he says.

"Are you kidding?"

"No."

"Oh, my God." Laurel is genuinely shocked.

"When Lucy was six months old, Issy went back to Los Angeles to fulfill her ambition of becoming an actress," Gerard said.

"What? She left her child?"

"Four years later she died."

It still felt uncomfortable to say her name in front of Laurel.

"That's crazy," Laurel says, "really crazy."

"That she died?" Gerard asks.

"Yeah, that, but for a mother to leave her child."

"It's what she did."

"I know, but it's crazy."

"Yeah."

"Did she ever visit?"

"No."

"Wow. I'm sorry, Gerard."

"It's okay. Lucy has no memory of her."

"But she was still her mother."

"Sure."

"Does she know?"

"No. I'll tell her when she is older, in high school maybe. I cannot bring myself to hurt her with the truth now. Something like that can destroy a child."

"You're still kind," she says.

"I love her, I'm her father. I want what's best for her."

"You were kind to me, too."

"Was I?" Gerard says. "I don't feel as if I was."

"You were," she says, "despite everything."

Gerard went to Issy's funeral in Los Angeles four years ago. She was found floating in a pool. She'd written Gerard's name as her next of kin. Los Angeles was seventy-five degrees and dry. The air-conditioning in his rental car smelled like candy. Issy had played the part of a psychic on a soap opera. People exchanged business cards at the buffet after the cremation. Gerard told Lucy he had to visit Hollywood on business. She wanted to come. Indira offered to sleep over and did. Gerard brought Lucy a present back. He wanted to buy many but stopped himself. He didn't want LA to have a special significance. He brought Indira a gift, too—a tote bag from MoCA with little birds on it and French writing. Lucy had asked about her mother recently. Gerard didn't know what to say. He was planning on going to a child psychologist to ask for advice.

Gerard met Issy a month after he met Laurel. A decade ago, Gerard had never met any of them.

Gerard vaguely remembers the feeling of being in love with Laurel and the desire to have sex with Issy. He knew that other men enjoyed the occasional partner outside of long-term relationships, and he wanted to try it. Issy was an incredible lover. She sprayed perfume on her thighs. She was uninhibited and never took her heels off, even after. Issy wasn't upset when Gerard told her that he was falling in love with Laurel. She laughed and then cried and told him she was pregnant. Gerard thought it was a joke. She was always telling lies. Then he felt something crack inside him because she wouldn't stop crying and he knew it was true. He told Laurel the next night, and she said she understood. A week later, Laurel broke it off in an e-mail.

Gerard agreed to move in with Issy.

Gerard still has Laurel's wristwatch at home in his bedside cabinet. She left it in his apartment eight years ago. Miraculously, the battery still works. Sometimes at night Gerard takes it out and falls asleep as it drips from his fingers.

Laurel is forty-three now. She is a senior editor of business books. She had a cat, but it died. Gerard buys some coffee and asks if they can walk together. Of course, she says, and then looks outside at the blizzard and laughs. She is wearing the same kind of heels Issy used to wear. As they leave the deli, there are people getting out of a taxi.

"Quick," Gerard says and they get in.

In the cab they talk about the president, their parents, and Laurel's brief marriage. She is divorced now, and her ex-husband is living with another man in Brooklyn Heights. She laughs, but Gerard can see she is disappointed.

When they get to her building, Gerard's nose starts bleeding. Night has fallen upon the city, but the snow isn't stopping.

"Oh, my God," Laurel says, and tips Gerard's head back. People watch them.

"Jesus, come inside, okay?" she says to Gerard.

"Okay," he says.

In the elevator they talk about their jobs. He can feel the blood clotting in his nose. Tiny fragments of snow have lodged in Laurel's eyelashes.

Upstairs, Gerard calls Indira to say he'll be back a little later. Then he and Laurel make love first in the kitchen and then in her bed. Her body is not as he remembers it. It is softer and somehow more pliable. Her toes seem perfect.

Her apartment smells of expensive scented candles. She makes coffee after. Her furniture is modern and gray. He feels somehow inside of her—held by her, and he remembers as a boy, swimming to the bottom of a thick pond in summer.

When he arrives home, Lucy jumps down from her chair and runs into his arms.

Gerard kneels and her weight becomes his.

"Why aren't you in bed, pebble?" Gerard says.

Indira appears in the doorway. "School is canceled tomorrow because of the snow, so I didn't think you'd mind if she waited up."

"Of course, Indira, it's perfectly fine."

"Why are you so late, Daddy?" She is kissing him all over his face. Gerard imagines her mother floating in the pool.

"I love you," he says.

"I love you, too, Daddy, but where were you?"

"I met an old friend and we had dinner," he says. Lucy can smell a lie a mile off.

"Is your old friend an old woman?" Lucy asks.

"Yes, how did you know?" Gerard laughs.

"A daughter knows," she says and runs back to the table, laughing and flailing her arms as though they are about to become wings.

Indira won't stay, so Gerard gives her more than enough cab money and thanks her for staying late. She kisses him on the cheek and he holds her. Her hair smells of onions.

After a bedtime story, Lucy asks if she can meet her father's friend.

"I think that would be nice," Gerard says. Lucy looks shocked, as if she'd expected him to say no. Children are difficult to read sometimes.

"Does she like ice cream?" Lucy asks.

"Yes, she eats it every day."

"Are you going to marry her?"

Gerard pauses. "Wait and see."

"Does she have any children my age?"

"I don't think so. Do you want her to?"

"Only if they're not boys."

She asks her father to sit on the edge of her bed until she falls asleep. He says yes, as always, but falls asleep first, as always. Soon they are both asleep.

The snow is blowing against the window.

The room glows with the breath of streetlight.

Around midnight, Gerard wakes up. Lucy stirs.

"Daddy, where's panda?" Gerard finds her stuffed panda and lays it next to her. She goes back to sleep immediately.

In the kitchen, Gerard pours himself half a tumbler of whiskey. He turns out the lights in the apartment, checks the front door, and then walks barefoot into his study.

Instead of taking down a book from the shelf, he looks out the window. He can see all the way up Lexington Avenue. The snow is drifting across the city in waves. Traffic is thin. A few glowing eyes.

He knows that before long Laurel will move in with them. He thinks of Issy. He remembers her laugh, then the roar of snapping flames at her cremation.

All of a sudden he feels a chill like cold water down his back. The tumbler of scotch slips from his fingers and shatters on the floor. Gerard spins around. His heart leaps into his throat. Someone was there, he could have sworn it. But in the space between him and the world he can see only air, only air and the auras of the day past and the day to come.

He thinks how strange life is with its frayed edges and second chances; and though by morning he will have forgotten that he ever thought it, Gerard feels as though he is being followed, that there are voices he can't hear, that the footsteps of snow on the window are just that, and like Lucy's conception—life is a string of guided and subtle explosions.

THE STILL BUT FALLING WORLD

I live in Rome where people sit by fountains and kiss. The sound of water is the sound of love rushing between them.

In the morning, the marketplace outside my apartment smells like artichokes. They grow on thick stalks. People forget they are flowers. Some leaves are the color of a blushing cheek. The hard leaves protect a heart.

Tomatoes are more delicate. The vines are laid in rows. Each vine bursts open in several places with a red fist.

The man who sells garlic comes from the south and doesn't sip coffee with the others at dawn. I watch him from my window. I, too, am from the south and know the loneliness of mornings.

Last week it was my cousin's son's birthday, and I sent a gift. I've been thinking a lot about my cousin lately. I'm starting to understand why she lied to us. She and her husband live with their children in the village where I grew up. It is called Morano Calabro, and the small stone houses wrap around the mountain like a cloak of many pockets.

At the top of the village are the ruins of a Norman castle where teenagers hide from their parents. It is always windy. They learn how to smoke and drink beer. They watch the drifting lights of cars in the valley. There's talk of moving to Naples, Rome, Venice, but most stay in the village and have beautiful children who grow quickly and want scooters.

Morano Calabro is about 500 kilometers south of Rome. In spring, it is common to see flocks of five or six butterflies. My father told me when I was a child that butterflies are just flowers that have come loose. Childhood was hard for me because I worried about everything. I worried about the end of the world, diabetes, earthquakes, asphyxiation, each of my family members slipping into a coma, one by one (as if going off to look for the others).

At age eight I would set my clock to rise in the early hours and check the regularity of my brother's breathing against my palm.

Life now is sometimes difficult, but at least I know that my condition is a condition and my concerns aren't always serious ones. I may not be normal, but I no longer worry about worrying, I just worry and know it's who I am. If you've never heard of such a thing, I'm surprised, as it's fairly common. You probably know someone who has it. Let me give you a recent example.

I was in a toy shop two weeks ago buying a present for my cousin's child. There was a box of lambs. I picked one up. The wool looked grubby, so I put it back and picked up another. Then the one I put back had this look. So I put the second lamb back to go with the first lamb (because I felt sorry for it), and the second lamb also had a look that said, for God's sake, can't you see I need love, too?

The shopkeeper was looking at me. "Can't decide, eh?" he said stupidly. I began to perspire. I looked around. On every shelf peering down at me were little heads, all pleading to be taken home and rescued from the darkness of a loveless existence. I almost slipped into a panic attack, which, if you've never had one, feels like you're free-falling in darkness (like Alice).

After twenty minutes, the shopkeeper said something else. I couldn't stand his looking and decided to buy them both. It was settled. I scooped them up in a moment of ecstasy and relief.

But two remained in the box. They both had looks. And one had a missing eye. I picked him up. I now had three lambs. There was one very lonely lamb left. He was very lonely. So alone he couldn't even look at me. And so I had all four sent in a box with the store's shiny wrapping paper and a sticker with their address on it. As he addressed the package, the shopkeeper asked me if Morano Calabro had a place to buy toys. "Of course," I said. You could tell he lived only for his shop.

My cousin's husband called during the birthday party a week later. There were children everywhere, he said. They were wearing paper crowns of different colors. I could hear them in the background, a jumble of soft, shallow voices. It's amazing to think they will age together, love one another, deceive one another, weep for each other, and in old age congregate at the public gardens and lock their arms. He put his son on the phone. "I'm three," he said. "Would you cry if I died?" "Yes," I said, and he blew me a kiss. I wonder if he thinks I'm really in the handset, tiny and groping.

The handset is sometimes like my body.

His father came on the phone. He wanted to know why four lambs. "Are they supposed to look the same?" he asked. "They don't look the same," I said. Then I told him they came as a set, which really wasn't a lie. "But why not three in a set like musketeers?" he asked. "Why not four," I said, "like the Ninja Turtles." "I suppose that makes sense," he said, having watched *Teenage Mutant Ninja Turtles* with his eldest boy that very morning. Never admit you have obsessive-compulsive disorder to someone who doesn't have it because they'll think you're crazy.

But the reason I'm telling you all this is because his wife, Isabella, who he thinks is my cousin, is not *really* my cousin. My entire family and her husband and children are living the most beautiful lie.

Her real name is not Isabella Ferrari, but Jocasta Lefferts. She's from Queens in New York City, and her last name is the name of the street she was found on by the local New York police. She came to my village five years ago. It was winter. She showed up and said her name was Isabella. She had a photograph of distant relatives, my grandmother's uncle, Luigi, and his wife, Luciana. Luigi was a metal craftsman. Luciana made clothes. She was partially sighted from birth. In 1917, Luigi's younger brother died in his older brother's arms from shrapnel wounds. Luciana waited for Luigi at the edge of the village to return from the war. When he did they walked to his mother's house in silence. His mother was outside hanging clothes. The sound of drops into dry earth, then footsteps. She turned around. It was the saddest-happiest day of her life.

Luigi and Luciana were soon married in an olive grove high above the village. The spot has not changed but for an old washing machine abandoned on the road halfway up the mountain. In 1920, they departed Morano Calabro for Argentina. No one knows anything about their lives after they left the village.

Isabella's Italian has improved over the past few years since she arrived from North America. From her look, I actually think her ancestors were West Indian, but that doesn't matter. She arrived with an elaborate story of how her grandmother (who was the daughter of Luigi and Luciana) married a Canadian soldier after World War II and moved to Toronto.

Isabella now has two children with a man from the village. She met him soon after arriving. He is handsome and wears Versace glasses. He works the village espresso machine at his newsstand. He dresses so fashionably tourists think he is from Rome or Milan. He is worldly without having gone anywhere, so nobody in the village was surprised when he married a stranger.

I think my grandmother knew Isabella was lying when she first came to the village five years ago. I wonder why she didn't say anything. She is a quiet woman. Her husband was older. When he was alive he worshipped her like a teenager.

My grandmother may know that Isabella is not really part of the family, but only I know her real name and her history (which is bleak). No, I would never say anything because everyone in the family (including her) is in love with one another.

She, her husband, and their two boys take a vacation once a year (nowhere special—Sicily or Bari), and at Christmas Isabella and her husband watch, from a sea of other parents, their children in the Nativity play, dressed in a patchwork of cloth and old carpet. I remember being on that stage dressed as a little bear. I was so nervous. I thought I was going to die out there and was sure that my outfit was teeming with fleas. After the play my father scooped me into his arms and I felt brilliant. For weeks, I felt brilliant. I even asked for a book on real bears.

Now I see it was such an insignificant event to the world. But then every beautiful moment in my life has been an insignificant event to the world.

Even though Isabella doesn't know it, I can relate to her. I know how it feels to be an outcast.

I left the village because I'm gay. And it's hard to be gay in a small place like Morano, even though it's beautiful and the streets smell of wood smoke, and you can go anywhere at anytime and you'll never be turned away by anyone. You must understand, it's a question of practicality, not a question of acceptance. Times have changed. In Morano, if you're loved, everything else falls away. My grandmother knows I fell in love with a man from Rome (the relationship has long since finished), and I pursued him here, which is where I've lived for four years.

Maybe I'll move back to the village in my twilight years. Perhaps I'll have a partner to take long, slow walks with. It's such a beautiful place. The Dutch artist M. C. Escher loved Morano. In 1930, he quietly made a woodcut of the village on Japanese paper. It hangs in the National Gallery of Canada.

We also have a fifteenth-century polyptych by Bartolomeo Vivarini in the main church, the skull of an old castle at the top of the village, a convent, ancient houses built into the mountain rock, and a public garden with a chuckling fountain where teenagers gather and explain the world to one another.

I wonder if Isabella suspects I know the truth about her. I don't have the courage to say anything, even if I could say I love you in the same breath. But then I don't see the point of truth anymore, it causes just as much heartbreak as lying.

Isabella told us five years ago when she arrived that her family was dead and that when she was going through her grandmother's things she found a photo with information written on the back.

She was actually in the village for two days before we met her. She arrived a few days before Christmas. Everyone was excited for the holiday, and it snowed through the night. The scent of trees blew down from the mountains in the morning, but by lunchtime this was replaced by the smells of baking, which spread through the streets like long fingers that pulled on everyone's tongues. Everyone had put up their decorations. You could sense the excitement of every child in the village, and they walked around in the evening with their eyes turned upward.

Isabella had taken a night train to Spezzano Albanese. After coffee and a croissant she hitchhiked to Castrovillari. The man who picked her up called his younger brother and asked him to drive Isabella to Morano Calabro. He had just worked a night shift and had to take his daughter to school. "She's from America and has come to find her family," he had said to his brother, which piqued the interest of their grandmother, who secretly listened in on her grandsons' conversations from an upstairs phone. The silence over dinner would be like cotton wool in the grandmother's mouth.

When Isabella arrived at the village it was the afternoon. She was cold and went to the village's grandest church, the Chiesa di S. Maria Maddalena. She fell asleep on a stiff pew. When she woke up, a man was sitting next to her. He had watery eyes. He asked her why she had come to the village.

She showed him the photograph of Luigi and Luciana. He hugged her. He explained that his own mother had died when he was six. He said it was like God had taken a bite out of him.

Isabella's Italian was very limited then. She didn't understand much that was said to her, but she hugged the man back. His sincerity made a deep impression.

Together, Isabella and the man with watery eyes went to the house of the local police inspector who had access to all the village records. He lived in a stone cottage on via Chiazzile. There was a pink plastic cup on his front step.

The man with watery eyes knocked. A man with white hair poked his head out of an upstairs window. "I'm trying to watch the news and my wife has a headache," he said. The man with watery eyes explained everything passionately. "One moment," the police inspector said, then closed the window.

In a few minutes, it began to snow. Then, the police inspector, dressed in full uniform, complete with medals he'd been awarded for bravery, quietly closed his front door and led them to the building where records were kept. The man with watery eyes pointed to the police inspector's medals and narrated the rescue of two boys from a frozen pond in the 1960s. Isabella asked where the brothers are now.

"Costa Rica," the police inspector said. "I just got a Christmas card from them."

At around three in the morning, the police inspector tapped a name in a dusty book. "I have found your family," he said. "I will call them at dawn." And the three of them sipped wine around the space heater until the sky turned white.

Isabella was kissed and hugged more than she had ever been in her life. The building of public records was a scene of great joy. The children of the family wondered what they would give her for Christmas. The man with watery eyes was the last to go home.

The day after Christmas, the police inspector and the man with watery eyes knocked on the family's door. The police inspector had his hat in hand. They had made a mistake, he said. They were not Isabella's real family.

There was anger and confusion. Isabella was summoned from an upstairs bedroom. One of the youngest children cried so hard it became his first memory.

She trudged back to the building that contained the public records. The wrong family followed. When my family arrived from the other side of the village, the wrong family eyed them jealously. Then the wrong family demanded to see the records for themselves. An unmarried uncle of the wrong family pointed out to my father that the police inspector had made one mistake, so was certainly capable of making a second. My father agreed this was a possibility.

Before leaving to come home with my family, Isabella promised the wrong family she would visit them and said kindly that you never know

who is who and that she was sure they were her family, too. My mother
agreed that God often did things like this for good reason.

I was in Naples visiting my uncle when all this happened and came
home the next day to find an American girl sleeping in my bed. My
English isn't bad, and I told her I didn't mind and then listened to my
mother's story of the mix-up and how the police inspector is really too
old to be in such a position of power. But then my father added that it
was all the police inspector had and to take his position would destroy
the man's spirit.

Isabella presented me with the photograph. Written on the back
were the names of my grandmother's uncle and his wife, the name of
the village, and the date they left. The photo was taken in an orchard.
Nobody knows where. Luciana is smiling in the photograph. "Perhaps
she was pregnant," I said. My grandmother looked at me sadly from
the kitchen as she dried her hands on a dish towel. Then she looked
at Isabella.

I'm going on a second date tonight. Marco is a restorer of Renais-
sance works, but he is really a sculptor. I met him on via Condotti.
We've sipped coffee together. His hands are beautiful.

It is quiet in my apartment as I pick out my clothes. I can hear the
future getting into position, like shuffling actors on a stage before the
curtain goes up.

Last night in bed, the idea of going out with Marco kept me awake.
My pillow must have soaked up a thousand conversations. Then I
imagined Marco choking on a piece of penne. Then I saw myself doing the Heimlich maneuver on him. But then I awoke from this half

sleep, this shallow river of worry, and realized that I don't even know the Heimlich maneuver, and had to go online at 3:00 a.m. and find out. Then I practiced in front of the mirror with a pillow.

This morning when I woke up I felt like a fool. I drank green tea and thought about Isabella as I watched the men in the market set out their day's vegetables and fruits. I then remembered the four lambs I had bought Isabella's son. One had a missing eye.

After Isabella had been with us a week, I decided to find out more about her because while looking in my room for something, I saw her passport poking out of her suitcase. I looked inside, and it said that it belonged to Jocasta Lefferts.

There was also a business card for a social worker. I wrote to her pretending to be the Italian authorities. I sent Isabella's passport as verification. It wasn't a very kind thing to do, but I was worried. Isabella didn't even realize the passport was missing. She hasn't left Morano since she arrived. The social worker I wrote to was assigned to an orphanage in Queens. She sent me a copy of Isabella's file. She had the file officially translated, but in clumsy guidebook Italian; the social worker had written, "Please take care of her" on the front of the file.

According to the file, an unnamed child was discovered by police in May of 1981 next to a Dumpster on Lefferts Avenue. As a teenager, she ran away several times from the center. She became a prostitute for two months to pay for her boyfriend's drugs. He died. She was beaten several times. There were other things, too. Terrible things.

After reading her file I began to love her. Whoever she is, I thought, she's now a member of the Ferrari family, and in the name of the Virgin Mary, I thought, we're claiming this child as one of ours (and I'm not even religious).

I rode my brother's bicycle up into the mountains and burnt her file along with her passport in the body of an old washing machine abandoned at the side of the road. There were wildflowers everywhere.

My grandmother saw I had received a package from America but said nothing. She and I are very close.

It is a beautiful evening, and I am walking through Rome to meet Marco. I am passing the Coliseum. I can imagine Marco waiting for me at the Piazza Navona beside the fountain of meeting rivers. There are tourists everywhere. They are taking pictures. I wonder what will happen to each photograph in the future. Strange to think photographs outlive us. The Roman Coliseum was once the scene of mass slaughter. People watched people being torn apart and crushed by wild animals from all over the world: lions, elephants, crocodiles, hippopotamuses. The Romans, the Romans. I can't stop thinking that everybody is somebody's child.

I once heard a guide explain to a spellbound crowd of tourists how when the Roman Empire fell, the Coliseum was abandoned and became overgrown with exotic plants and flowers, the seeds for which had been carried in the feces of animals brought from Africa, Asia, and Europe.

I'm now walking through the Roman Forum. If you ever come to this magnificent city, you'll be delighted to learn that it's all free. And bring your children, Italians love children. They'll be treated much better than you and given things to nibble on in every shop.

There are men strolling around dressed as gladiators. They will take a photo with you for a price. They play their parts well. Perhaps they really feel like Roman soldiers. Maybe they tell their wives over supper they were born too late.

I wonder if things can happen too early or too late or if everything happens at exactly the right time. If so, how sad and beautiful.

I'm almost at the Piazza Navona, which is where I'm meeting Marco. The alleys are choked with tourists. I'm tired. I haven't slept, remember. The sky is the color of a peach. It's evening, but it looks like morning. Every moment is a beginning and an end.

Isabella's children will never know their mother's sadness. It would destroy them because she is their mother and you only get one mother in this world. The thing I think about most is why she chose us. It would *seem* obvious to say that she is the lucky one, but I'm not sure it isn't the other way around. Her children's laughter falls through open windows into the village street. The man she married is deeply in love. I wonder if he bit his lip when he first saw her.

I am taking a shortcut. I am threading my way through secret alleys. There are dogs lying perfectly still. There are bags of trash and empty oil canisters. There are waiters smoking with their shirts unbuttoned. *Ciao* they say because I smile at them first. I think most people in the world are decent if they're not suffering.

It was hard for me to leave the house tonight. I couldn't stop checking the gas knobs. They were all off, and there was no hissing sound, but I just couldn't stop looking. And then I checked all the plug sockets and listened to the toilet in case something unseen was overflowing. And then when I did finally leave, I had to try the door handle ten times, just to make sure. The whole door is coming loose, but then if I leave the apartment three times a day, that's 210 times per week the handle gets jiggled. Maybe Marco could tighten it up for me. I can see his hands upon the hinges like two horses.

My neighbor is used to the sound of me jiggling the lock. If I were ever being broken into, she'd never suspect. I buy her a bottle of wine every now and then. I wish she could find someone.

I wonder if Isabella found the photograph of our family in a thrift store in New York City. Perhaps the real Isabella gave it to her on her deathbed.

The mystery is how the photograph traveled from Argentina to New York.

It took only moments for Isabella's husband to fall in love with her. And only a few moments for Isabella's biological mother to set her down on the street and walk away forever. Perhaps, desperately, her mother now has something to hope for. Like a lighthouse, her child missing in the world is a light diffused by the fog of her own despair; a despair beyond sadness.

Isabella's real mother felt her only power was to give up on everything, like Pontius Pilate washing his hands before the hot crowd. But her child went searching, and on a quiet Italian mountainside she found a future waiting for her.

I think we keep these moments of rejection and acceptance very close. I think we carry them always, like cracked shells from which a part of us once hatched.

I see Marco in the distance. He is holding two oranges. I can feel him without touching him. I stop walking. I want this moment never to end. I want to hold on in this still but falling world.

He sees me. We walk toward each other.

Sometimes the man with watery eyes calls on Isabella. She always asks him in. Her children sit on his lap and feed him little pieces of biscotti. They want to hear the story of the church, they want to hear the story of mama. They want to know everything.

ACKNOWLEDGMENTS

I wish to directly acknowledge these people:

Darren Booy (for knocking on the wall), Joan Booy, Dr. Stephen Booy, Ken Browar, Sandra Buratti, Justine Clay, Christine Corday, Lindsay Edgecombe, Danielle Esposito, Patricio Ferrari, Peggy Flaum, León García, Francis Howard, Lucas Hunt, P.K., Dr. Mickey Kempner, Hilary Knight, Bénédicte Le Lay, Laura Lyons, Michael Matkin, Mary McBride, Anne Michaels, Dr. Edmund Miller of Long Island University, Samuel Morris III, Dr. William Neal of Campbellsville University, Jonathan D. Rabinowitz, Sheridan Sansegundo, Paula Sinnott, Jessamyn Tonry, Keith Usher, F.C.V., Lorilee Van Booy, Wim Wenders, Peter Handke, and Jurgen Knieper for *Wings of Desire*, Dr. Barbara Wersba, and the Russo family of Morano Calabro, Italy.

I also wish to acknowledge:

Greenpoint Café

Humanities Department at the School of Visual Arts, New York

Musée de la Résistance Nationale, Paris

Shakespeare and Company, Paris

Wellspring House, Massachusetts

Printed in the United States
145608LV00008BA/128/P

9 781933 527055